NINE WORLDS WEST

By
PAUL W. FAIRMAN

ARMCHAIR FICTION
PO Box 4369, Medford, Oregon 97504

*For more information about Armchair Books and products, visit our
website at…*

www.armchairfiction.com

Or email us at…

armchairfiction@yahoo.com

PERMANANTLY TRAPPED ON A PLANET OF DEATH

Greta Lansing wanted ex-space pilot Cort Leggitt to fly her to the planet Pentar in search of her kidnapped father. She had heard through the space grapevine that Leggitt had nerves of steel and could fly in and out of any planetary system. But Leggitt had been blacklisted by the Pilot's Guild the year before after a freak jet backfire accident had left five of his clients burned to a crisp. However, Lansing's money—and her overwhelming beauty—had been more than enough to coax him back into the pilot's seat. After navigating through one of the worst asteroid fields in the galaxy, Greta's party found themselves crash-landed on a planet ruled by a brazen Earth-born gangster and his tall alien henchmen. But with the help of two six-legged Martian tigers, along with the blind allegiance of a multitude of hairless alien pygmies, Greta Lansing soon found her status changed from space fugitive to planetary divinity.

FOR A COMPLETE SECOND NOVEL, TURN TO PAGE 99

CAST OF CHARACTERS

CORT LEGGITT

After being blacklisted by the Guild he seemed content to drink his life away—but then a dark-haired beauty walked into his life.

GRETA LANSING

She had come to Pentar to rescue her kidnapped father. Little did she know that she would soon become a goddess.

BUTCH MECROPOLIS

Being greatly overweight didn't exactly do wonders for his love life, but he did have the unflinching loyalty of two Martian tigers!

BOSS HAGERTY

He reigned supreme over an entire outlaw planet, but in truth he wasn't much more than your average street thug from Chicago.

KORBO

Hagerty's number one thug—and vicious to the core when so ordered. But this tall alien was essentially a coward at heart.

JOHN LANSING

He had once been a big, well-accomplished space pilot, but now he was little more than bones and hideously mottled skin.

SAM FRENCH

He looked like he should be designing lady's hats rather than checking the jet temperature and atom power of a spaceship.

MAGGIE AND MIKE

These six-legged Martian tigers could tear a human to shreds, yet they were strangely loyal to a fat man and a beautiful woman.

CHAPTER ONE

THE GIRL said, "I'm looking for a man."

Cort Liggett glanced up from his drink and grinned briefly without humor.

"I don't think you'll have much trouble finding one, sister," he said. "Not with the equipment you've got there."

She was exceptionally tall, willowy, and had hair as dark as the seventh sin. She hadn't been speaking to Cort, but rather to Butch Mecropolis, the adventurous Greek who'd come to Mars with the first ship load of emigrants from Earth, in order to establish a liquor house in New Portland where even a discredited pilot could run up a tab.

Her assertion had been heard also by a blond Martian down the bar who liked the ways and the women of Earth people and frequented their city. The Martian got to his feet and came forward, swaggering. "I'm a man, honey. Let's go."

Cort said, "Not the right one though, sonny," and then got off his stool and hit the Martian in the softest spot Martians have—the belly. The Martian folded-up and forgot about women as Cort helped him to the door and booted him into the street.

Butch said, "You're damn free and easy with my cash customers. That stuff they carry doesn't grow on trees."

Cort looked a trifle hurt. "I was doing you a favor, Butch. Hit a Marty in the belly, he gets sick. You don't want your floor all dirtied up, do you?"

Cort went back to his drink and Butch Mecropolis turned again to the girl. "What were you saying, miss?"

"I'm looking for a man they told me I might find here. His name is Cort Liggett. He's a pilot."

Cort glanced up again. "Correction," he said. "An ex-pilot. Sit down and I'll buy you a drink."

Butch snorted. "I never saw a guy so open handed with other people's liquor." He moved down the bar a bit, motioning the girl to follow. "What'll you have?"

"A small Lazant. Is this man Cort Liggett?"

"Give her a large Lazant," Cort said. Then to the girl: "Take the load off, babe. The stools are soft and the company leaves nothing to be desired. What's on your mind?"

She sat down and stared at him thoughtfully. "You're a little drunk, aren't you?"

"About as drunk as I can get lately. I used to do much better, but I guess I'm slipping."

"Are you sober enough to talk business?"

"What kind of business?"

"I need a pilot."

CORT straightened with mock dignity. "Madam, I think you should know exactly with whom you are conversing. Cort Liggett is the name. A has-been. A washed-up hot shot. A character black-listed permanently by the Guild of Space Pilots for losing his ship in the Asteroids. Let's have another drink and I'll tell you more." He reached toward his glass but didn't make it. His head went smack down on the bar and he was out.

Butch Mecropolis was there to catch the glass before it went over. "He drinks more than he should," Butch said apologetically, "but it was pretty bad. He saw five of his friends fried to a crisp in a jet backfire. It was a hunting party he took up in the Asteroids—guys he knew. They got drunk and snuck into the pilot room while he went for coffee. They gummed up the controls and got roasted to death for playing around. He didn't really lose the ship. He brought it in on one jet. The bodies of five pals he delivered to the space port in a crippled ship—a job one pilot in a thousand could do. But the Guild made an example of him because it was an unscheduled flight. I think why he drinks is he keeps seeing his friends the way he found them in the control room."

The girl lifted Cort's head and laid it in a more comfortable position on the bar. "I heard about that affair. In fact, I checked into it very carefully. I'm interested only in the part about his being a hot pilot. Where I'm going, I'll need one."

"I can sober him up in a jiffy," Butch said eagerly. "I got some stuff'd wake up a stone statue."

She shook her head. "It can wait until he sobers up. Where does he stay?"

"Palmer Hotel around the corner. Room 601."

The girl got off her stool, lifted Cort expertly. She got her arm around his waist and draped one of his over her shoulders. "I'll take him home," she said. Then, at Butch's look of surprise: "I can handle him alright. I had plenty of experience with my father."

She took Cort to his room and dumped him on the bed. She took his shoes off and then curled up in a chair and went to sleep.

WHEN SHE told him her name was Greta Lansing, he groaned and said, "As long as you're here, go on out and get some coffee. You'll need to make sure it's black and strong. That damn Greek melts dynamite and calls it liquor."

She went without a word, and when she came back he said, "I think I've heard of you. Or your father at least. Didn't he run a black ship* into the forbidden zones up Orion way?"

Greta Lansing nodded. "Dad staked everything on being able to bring a load of thradium back to the Solar markets. He'd lost five fortunes in the space trade and he wanted to get one more and retire. We went to Pentar, out beyond the boundaries."

Cort frowned. "Pentar—"

"That's the oversize asteroid they nick-named 'Boss Hagerty's planet.' It's beyond Orion, through a bad asteroid belt."

"Beyond the boundaries. You know, the Interplanetary Council had a damn good reason for declaring that area out of bounds. It's too far to extend diplomatic protection. Anyone who—"

"I know all about that. But we went anyhow. Sank almost our last dime in a cargo of heavy salt—it's priceless out there. But Boss Hagerty turned his hatchetman on us; a devil named Korbo who stole the load and held Dad as a hostage for another one."

CORT FROWNED. "Those people must be crazy. If they paid you well, they should have known you'd bring another cargo."

---

* A black ship: One unlisted on Space Authority records and thus not given service by a guild pilot.

"They were afraid not, but there was something more than that. You know how they hate us—love to get their hands on Inner Planetary people. There are stories—"

"I've heard some of them." He took the cold towel off his head and regarded the girl with frankly appraising eyes. She had a tanned, flawless complexion. Her long legs clad in skin-tight space-pants were lush and perfect. She had as beautiful a body as Cort had ever seen. "It's strange this Korbo didn't hold you and send your father back for more salt."

She did not flush under his gaze. She took his eyes and words in a manner indicating her matter-of-fact attitude toward all things, from sex to forbidden space travel. "Dad's reputation is pretty well known, even in the far galaxies. Korbo would have liked to have had me, but the salt was more important, and he was afraid Dad would get drunk and forget all about it."

"You're dad's probably having a hard time of it out there."

"There's no doubt about it."

"How did you get clear of the bad areas without him?"

"Korbo is no mean pilot himself. He piloted us to open void and then went back."

"And now you want a non-guild pilot to take you in again with another load of salt to buy your dad back."

"I want a hot pilot. That's why I hunted you up."

"But it's silly. They didn't keep their word the first time. Why should it be any different now?"

"It probably won't be."

"Then why go back? Korbo would take you this time."

"I've got to go back anyhow."

"Do you know what those men out there do to Inner Planetary women, and not just the beautiful ones either—any female from the solar planets?"

"I know. But I've got to chance it. I've got to go back with a load of heavy salt and try to get Dad out of their hands. I think you ought to come with me."

"Why?"

"What have you got to lose?"

"Only my life."

"You're losing that here. You're killing yourself as fast as you can right now. You ought to come, because you'll be a lot happier dying out there. It would be a much cleaner death."

He'd been sitting on the edge of the bed. He got to his feet and reached for her. "The hangover's about gone. So much so, that you're damned attractive to me. I'd be a fool not to kiss you."

She got up and moved toward him. "And I'd be a fool not to let you, if it would help." She knew how to make a kiss further her cause. A long minute later, he pushed her back. "You weren't just promoting. You liked that."

"Of course I liked it, but I was promoting just the same. Will you go?"

"I'll go alone. You stay here. I'll be back."

"You couldn't get the ship out of berth alone. You're not a guild pilot."

"Neither are you."

"But I'm listed as owner of the Space Wagon, and I've got pilot's papers. I don't have to be Guild."

"All right. We'll start that way and then I'll drop you somewhere to wait."

She kissed him again and another minute passed. "Once I get on the ship—I'll stay."

"WE GO SPACESIDE tomorrow at dawn," Cort said.

Butch Mecropolis reached for a bottle of Lazant and three glasses. "I'll miss you—both of you. We'll drink to clear void and a fast trip."

"For the three of us."

"What are you talking about?"

"We want you to come, Butch. If we hit, it means a country house and eight servants. You always wanted to be rich."

Greta Lansing said, "I have a crew. A good engine room man who will make the trip and three able tube scrapers, but they wouldn't be worth much in case of trouble. Cort says you're a man to have around in a pinch."

"He does, huh?" Butch poured the drinks, frowning the while. "You said how it would be if we hit. How about a miss?"

"It wouldn't be so good, but we won't talk about that," Cort replied.

"Not a chance. I couldn't leave my cats."

Cort turned to Greta. "I didn't tell you. Butch has got the only trained Martian pussies in existence."

"Not the big ones."

Butch grinned with pride. "Yeah, the big six-legged ones. Got hold of them when they were three-foot kittens. They're eight feet long now, and one of them has twelve inch fangs." Butch's black eyes softened. "You ought to hear 'em purr."

"Sounds like all the dynamos in the city power plant," Cort said, "but they're pretty cats."

"I'd like to go, but I couldn't leave them. They'd pine away and die."

"You could take them along," Greta said.

Butch was tempted. "Have you got room for their food? They'd need at least five horse carcasses for the trip."

"We'll make room."

"I'll think it over."

Cort got off his stool. "Fine. Be at Number Five Berth at the space field tomorrow before sunup."

"I said I'd think it over."

"Do that. I'll see the horse meat is aboard. See you later."

"You take a hell of a lot for granted," Butch growled.

From the door, Cort called back: "And see you lock this joint up tight, I want to find it the same when we get back."

After Cort and Greta left, Butch prowled up and down the bar talking out loud to himself. "It'd be nice to have money. Maybe then I could afford a job like that dark-haired honey. That would be something." Then, he looked in the bar mirror and his ugly face turned sad. "No. No dame would go for my pan, even for all the cash in the System." He picked up the three empty glasses. "Only my cats love me," he sighed, and mopped the bar with a rag.

CHAPTER TWO

ON THE following morning, two six-legged tigers, large enough to lift and carry a Martian hill buffalo, slithered through the dark streets of New Portland toward the space port. Each wore a solid silver collar to which were attached silver chains. The chains tinkled in the cold morning air, and more than one early riser fled panic stricken through the alleys and away.

Butch Mecropolis leaned backward on the chains and slid along on his heels. He could tell by the tone of the deep growls that his cats were happy. "Relax, babies," he crooned, the fat on his gross body bouncing like jelly at every step. "Papa's taking you for a ride among the stars. Maybe you'll find out what Pentarian meat tastes like. Come good luck, maybe you can eat Boss Hagerty. Wouldn't that be something?"

At the space port, the entrance guards stepped aside fast and with the minimum of dignity. "They won't hurt you as long as I say not to." Butch called out cheerily. But the guards were already quite a distance away and probably didn't hear.

Cort was waiting at the ramp. "About time," he growled. "We've been waiting ten minutes. Take them through into the after housing. Put them in the cabin next to the meat. And whatever you do, be sure to lock the door!"

"They're good cats," Butch replied. "House broken and everything. Give 'em a ton or so of sand, and they won't dirty up the floor a bit. They're clean by nature."

The cats dragged Butch on into the ship and Cort turned to see Greta hurrying back from the clearance office. She was folding a paper and tucking it into her blouse. Her red lips were parted slightly, her eyes bright as the void-fires off Mercury. "Clearance granted," she said.

"Then this is it."

For a moment, as she passed him up the ramp, her face was close to his. "This is it, and thanks, Cort Liggett."

"Don't mention it. Get aboard and lift her."

After the ports were secured and the jets fired, Cort stood beside her as she leaned forward from the pilot's chair. "Do you know how to get one of these crates spaceside without breaking every back on board?" he asked.

"Just watch me. You won't even have to sit down. Just hold onto the chair."

From the speaker came the voice from Port Control: "Jet away on eleven." A bell struck a single note and Greta's eyes were glued to the big red hand on the clock. Under the light blouse, Cort looked down the contour of her rich bosom—saw the breasts rise and fall. He thought how lovely they were, and then a muffled rearward roar nudged the Space Wagon down the five-mile berth-chute, and a blue light flashed on to indicate the ship was no longer earthbound. "Nice," Cort told her. "A little too fast on the right jets, but still nice."

"Thank you, sir. Count ten."

IN THE next ten seconds, the Space Wagon pointed her sleek nose into the heavens and shook off the last pull of gravity with a disdainful flip of her white-hot jets.

"Ten," Cort said.

Greta slid out of the pilot's seat.

"Your ship, darling. Be good to her and she'll respond. Please don't knock her nose off on any uncharted solids."

"I'll do my best."

"I'm going to cry, damn it."

"Why?"

"Because yesterday there was so little hope—so much nothing. And now you're here—and Butch with his six-legged cats."

"They'll eat us out of house and home."

"This is one of my helpless moments. I get that way. Right this minute, you could have anything you asked for."

"And me in a pilot's chair. Beat it. I've got to plot course."

Greta went away and Cort sat for a long time in the chair with all the gauges before him. There were one hundred and seven of them and he knew each one—not just from knowledge, but from an instinct that told him when any one of them would go wrong even when they were right. For a moment, he sat back and closed his eyes.

Once a pilot has coursed a thradium hull through void on hot jets, he is never the same. It is the feeling a pilot gets after the first flush of stage fright; it is the blending of space and blood when the void takes a man over; the wedding of flesh and bone and mind and soul to the magnetic nothingness which is the last great barrier between man and God. It is the supreme moment given to a few men when they get that wild, free feeling of immortality.

Cort's heart pounded hard as he remembered the moment of his first takeoff years before. The little ceremony after lessons were learned, tests passed and this was it; after so many had fallen from the hopeful ranks and only a few were left and he was one of them. The C.O. of the

Guild gave him his ship at the top of the ramp by the open port. The C.O. pinned his shield on, shook hands and then became human. The words that were traditional—the last words: "Heaven's up there somewhere, boy. Go find it."

Yes, there was something about piloting a spaceship that got a man. I'm back again, Cort thought. Back in a pilot's chair. We'll see if I've got the old touch.

AN HOUR later, Sam French came in from the engine room. He was a small, fine-featured man who looked as though he should be designing lady's hats rather than checking the temperature of jets and keeping atom power evenly distributed. He could have reported over the intercom, but he wanted to size up the pilot, and the pilot was glad because he wanted to size up French.

"How's the distribution?"

"Good," French said. "Number Three is lagging about five hundred degrees. I'm timing it for wash now. May have to scrape it."

"When do you think we can open up?"

"In about five hours, I'd say."

Cort whistled. "I've known ships that took twelve hours to heat."

"This is a good ship."

"Fine. Let me know when you're ready."

"I will." French turned toward the door, then hesitated: "About those cats," he said.

"Not as bad as they look."

"I'm glad of that. I wouldn't care to be torn up and eaten." But French still looked doubtful as he left the pilot room, and Cort decided he wouldn't be much help if trouble came. And he felt sure trouble would certainly come.

The Space Wagon picked up gradually to four thousand on its own increased heat during the next two hours. Cort spent the time in intensive concentration on the plotting board. Satisfied, finally, he straightened and ran a hand though his thick, unruly hair. He stood for a minute, frowning. There was a restlessness, an urge within him that he couldn't analyze immediately. Then, a pair of dark eyes and slim hips arose in imagery before him, and he knew.

He paced swiftly up and down the control room. Hell! Her attitude, her manner, had been practically an invitation. Of this he was pretty sure. But even if he was wrong, she would never be in a more cooperative mood. Why not take advantage of it?"

His conscience hastened to tell him that this was poor sportsmanship, but he scowled his conscience down. After all, she was no callow school girl. Probably not even a virgin. She'd been around and knew what made men tick. No doubt, she was wondering what held him back. Hadn't she said he could have anything he asked for?

Cort went out into the central passageway and up-ship toward the captain's quarters. He stood for a moment, then knocked resolutely on her door. She called "Come in," instantly, and he found the door unlocked.

INSIDE, HE found nothing very feminine. It was a neat, comfortable cabin, but Cort got the impression she hadn't changed a thing since she'd taken it over.

Greta wore a dark blue robe of simple cut over the collar of which billowed the dark glory of her hair. Her face was washed clean of makeup and possessed a shininess that gave her the look of a little girl.

She got up from the lounge upon which she'd been lying and smiled at Cort. "How goes the ship, pilot?"

"Jet's heating. Full speed in about three hours."

"So soon? Wonderful. Can I make you a cup of tea?"

Cort stepped forward. Greta stood waiting for him.

Breast to breast, they stared into each other's eyes. She made no move, gave no indication of either approval or disapproval. He raised his arms slowly and drew her close to him. She did not resist. He kissed her and her lips were warm, even though she did not raise her arms nor press herself forward. Somewhat doubtfully, he released her.

There was a little fright in her eyes now as she looked up at him, a slight trembling of her body when she said, "You want me, don't you?"

"Yes."

"Badly?"

"Very badly."

"Do you want me to tell you how it is, or do you just want to barge right ahead?"

"Tell me."

"It's this way. You're something pretty special in more ways than one. In what you are and what you've done for me, and you can have me if you want me. If it must be now, I'll promise to cooperate and do my best to see that you're pleased. I may even enjoy it myself. But it won't be the great good thing it could be, because I'll be a little broken hearted about it. You see, being a healthy, normal animal, I've always dreamed about what it would be like, but in the first part of the dream there has always been a man with his collar on backwards, a ring slipping on my finger and a husband whispering in my ear about loving me very much. As I said, Cort, I'll do my best, but it will no doubt be with tears in my eyes."

He had dropped his arms and backed away from her. He stared at her and he had never in his life seen anyone he wanted more. He turned abruptly toward the door. As he fumbled for the knob, he said, "Full speed in three hours."

"Cort."

"Yes."

"Kiss me."

"You go to hell…"

WITH A SOFT cry, she brushed forward and turned him and drew him down. There was fire on his lips coming from hers, and words she whispered against his teeth while she, spoke: "Darling, am I ungrateful? A stinking sport?"

He grinned at her. "Honey, Butch's Martian kitties can eat a horse between them in a few gulps—but they've got nothing on you." He went out and closed the door.

Some three hours later, Sam French's voice came over the intercom. "Tubes at peak heat. Any time you're ready, Mr. Liggett."

"No time like the present," Cort replied. He dropped into the pilot chair and opened the loudspeaker. "To all aboard. Get set for top speed. Butch, hold on to those damned cats. Here we go."

He set himself to the controls and the ship trembled and a low rumble was heard from the tubes. He pressed and the tubes whined like a child in agony. Then, the great ship seemed to come alive. It rocked on its axis as the thradium nose split void with a hundred times its previous force.

Each minute the ship appeared to have reached its capacity, but the next minute found it traveling ever faster until the child whine changed to hopeless wailings of a thousand devils in everlasting fire. This, it seemed, was more than metal could stand, but still the Space Wagon increased its speed.

A few minutes later Cort got out of his chair, just as the door opened and the scared white face of Butch appeared. "How the hell fast is this butter boat traveling?" he asked.

"Slightly less than half a light year a day," Cort told him.

"What are the chances of its blowing up?"

"About one in ten. The odds are far in our favor."

"My poor kitties. They didn't ask to come on this suicide dash. We ought to be ashamed of ourselves, putting them in danger."

"Give them an extra horse for breakfast. A little reward for good behavior." Cort grinned, set the automatic pilot, and followed Butch into the passageway.

Came the time, days later, when Greta entered the pilot room and laid her hands on Cort's shoulders as he sat tense in his chair. He had not moved for over nine hours now, and Greta said, "Don't you think you should get a little sleep now?"

Cort watched the radar screen with burning eyes, eternally on the alert for the wandering asteroids that could hurtle out of nowhere straight for the nose of the Space Wagon. "Your pappy," Cort said, "was a hot pilot, honey. So was Korbo, if he brought you through this rock pile without a busted hull."

Three times in as many hours, Cort had saved the ship from annihilation by a feather touch on the jet controls. His mouth was a tight line and his face haggard. But now he loosened a trifle and laid his hand on that of Greta. "I think we're coming into the clear, though. They're thinning out. Try getting some rest yourself."

Greta smiled wearily, went to her cabin and dropped exhausted into her bunk. But only to be awakened within the hour by Cort's voice on the intercom: "All passengers—alert for disaster! Alert for disaster !"

CHAPTER THREE

GRETA HURRIED down the passageway to find Sam French wringing his hands in the pilot room. "There was absolutely no reason why the tube should blow, Mr. Liggett. It was cleaned less than three hours ago."

Cort turned to Greta as she entered. "Number Four jet tube backfired. The tube-scrapers were burned to a crisp."

Greta went pale under her rich tan. "All...three men?"

"Never knew what hit them. We're in trouble. So near and yet so far." Butch Mecropolis entered in time to hear Cort's words. "How bad trouble?" Butch asked.

"We're clear of the heavy asteroid fields and bearing on Pentar. But the tube scraping equipment is melted down to a puddle. With the jet wash piling up, she'll go in like a kite in a high wind. We either let gravity take her and hope for the best, or pull away and explode in space."

"There really isn't much to decide, is there?" Greta asked.

"Of course not," Cert snapped. "We go in."

"How long will it be?" Butch wanted to know.

"About an hour."

Butch grinned weakly. "Then we'll find out how hot a pilot you really are."

"Won't we, though," Cort answered. He turned to Greta. "You'd better get dressed, unless you want to land with your legs showing."

Greta left the room and Sam French said, "I'll go back to the engine housing and do what I can."

"You stay away from those jets. We've lost enough men."

"Yes, sir," French said meekly, and there was relief in his voice.

"I gotta see about my cats," Butch said. French followed him out and Cort was alone.

Cort stared sourly at the radar plate. It was practically clear now except for the faint signal from Pentar. No doubt the Space Wagon was also registering on the landside equipment of the small planet. Possibly escort ships had already been dispatched to bring the big ship in.

They're going to wonder no end about our antics from here on in, Cort thought. That is, if they can keep us in range. Cort took a few turns around the room. Maybe, he told himself, it's just as well if they lose us. We might live longer that way.

Twenty minutes later, he told the group assembled behind his chair. "We're inside gravity. Prayers are now in order."

SILENTLY, they watched him play lightly with the controls, flirt with the last bit of power left in the smothered jets. The ship nosed upward and described a fantastic five-hundred mile arc, stood for a moment on her jets, then reversed and dived straight toward the gravity center.

Sweat stood out on Cort's forehead. Another such arc would kill the jets completely and the Space Wagon would come to rest possibly a hundred feet under the surface of Pentar. The glide would have to be made at exactly the right second. Then, if there was enough power in the tubes to respond, and if there were no mountains in the way, the Space Wagon might have a fifty-fifty chance of coming in without killing all on board.

Cort's eyes ached as he stared into the radar plate and watched Pentar rocket toward them. He surveyed the terrain swiftly. The soil seemed a scant inch from his teeth when he pressed the ship into a glide and tried to remember a prayer he'd learned as a child. He didn't recall the prayer, but the Space Wagon leveled sluggishly off, the ground loomed large, and Cort threw himself to the floor directly across Greta's body. Her lips were against his cheek and she whispered, "I'm sorry, darling, about not letting you—"

The little world of the Space Wagon was torn to pieces by a bone-splintering crash.

They piled up like cordwood against the cushioned forward wall of the ship. For a time, they did not breathe nor think, but only lay tense waiting for death. There was a great silence after the rending sounds died.

Then, Cort's clipped voice: "All right! We made it. Now…are we trapped in this cheese box for good?"

Sam French's muffled voice was hopeful: "I don't think she turned over. We're still on the floor."

"I wonder how my cats came out?" Butch said.

Greta's soft breast was directly under Cort's protecting hand. "Are you all right?" he asked.

"I think so. Let's see about the doors."

Cort led the way into the passage and tried the pneumatic switch. It worked. There was a hiss of air and the door opened outward. Cort jumped to the ground and turned to catch Greta as she followed. With a slight grin on his face, he asked, "What was it you said just as we crashed?"

Greta flushed and turned her head away. "I didn't say a word. You must have been hearing things." Cort released her with the thought that he'd seen her blush for the first time.

French leaped down to reveal a badly sprained wrist, which Cort bound with a handkerchief. "Looks as though we came through pretty good," Cort said. "Where's Butch?"

The answer came as one of the great fanged cats poked its head out and leaped smoothly to the ground, followed by its mate. Then, Butch's moon face appeared.

THE CATS snarled and circled off to the left where they crouched side by side, snapping their tails and digging their fangs into the soil.

"Easy babies." Butch crooned. He jumped down and approached them fearlessly to snap the silver chains into their collars. Crooning wordlessly, he led them back toward the ship. "Not a scratch on either one."

Cort was staring at the Space Wagon with a look of bitterness in his eyes. "Meet a hot pilot," he said, his voice heavy with self-contempt. "Maybe I didn't really lose that other ship, but the Guild merely anticipated. There's no doubt about this one."

"You got us in," French said. "Few pilots could have done that."

"I wasn't fishing for compliments. Does anybody know where the hell we are?"

Greta, seemingly unaware of her action, was stroking the head of one of the cats. The beast growled deep in its throat, quivered and sank down at her feet. Butch grinned. "What do you know about that? Maggie likes you. She never took to anybody before. You must have a way with cats."

"I've studied maps of Pentar," Greta told Cort. "It looks to me as though we've come down in the Gormal Desert. If I'm right, there should be heavy forests somewhere south of here. Korbo has lumber camps in the forest he runs with slave labor. The planet's only large city is about ninety miles away."

"Hagerty City, isn't it?"

"That's right. The spot from where Boss Hagerty runs the planet. And he'll be looking for us, of course. We must have registered on his radar."

"No doubt of that." Cort motioned toward Butch. "Come on, Lard. Let's get the space cars out. I don't care much for this God-forsaken section."

Butch followed Cort back into the ship, protesting the while. "Don't call me Lard, I'm not so fat. Just plump and well upholstered."

"Get a hold."

Together, they brought the small, compact cars, one at a time, out onto the ground. Cort crushed the inflation capsules, and immediately rubber frames were blown up to form seating space for three persons in each car.

Cort returned again to the ship and came back with four gun harnesses, each holstering two efficient spectrum guns and one hundred rounds of ammunition.

CHAPTER FOUR

SCARCELY had the group buckled on the weapons, when a low humming sound turned all eyes to the southwest. The humming increased until a low-flying car raised a rocky butte in that direction and came into view.

It was an antique, outmoded affair, but was handled with efficiency as it circled, seemingly for a landing. It swung low toward the crippled spaceship, and four men could be seen riding the platform.

"The tall one," Greta said. "It's Korba himself! What will we do, Cort?"

"Do?" Cart shrugged, his narrowed eyes on the space car. "What is there to do? Wait and see what happens."

Things happened speedily. Instead of landing, the car swerved sharply and came back with its deck tilted toward the four Earthlings. Cort's reaction was instantaneous. He yelled, "Take cover!" and caught Greta's arm and hurled her roughly into the shelter of the Space Wagon's bulging hull. Butch, standing a few yards away between his cats, dropped to the ground as the Pentarian space car spat a tube of green flame toward the big ship.

Cort's two guns were in action instantly. As the lethal green fire struck Sam French, smashing him into a lifeless pulp, Cort poured two answering streams of heat pellets toward the attackers. One of the ancient car's metal fins melted and dropped away in a stream of molten metal. There was a quick scream from the gunner above as he straightened in a frenzy of agony and pitched to the ground.

"The dirty swine!" Cort grated.

"They planned to kill us in cold blood! Cut us down like animals! Evidently they didn't expect resistance."

The Pentarian car had swept on by and was circling for another rush. Butch, his face ashen, was erect now and running toward the spaceship hull. He labored mightily, hauling his cats behind him, but still found voice to protest, "The dirty bums. They're trying to clean us out! And they got French! What the hell kind of hospitality is this?"

"Boss Hagerty's kind," Cort said, eyes on the Pentarian ship, guns poised for another shot. Then, he quickly holstered the weapons. "They're in trouble. They can't turn with that bad fin. We've got to get aloft and outdistance them. Get your cats into one of the cars, Butch. I'll cover you, and then we'll follow in the other car. Get going!"

As Butch pulled the great beasts toward the nearer car, Greta sprang from the shelter of the hull. "Cover us both," she called out. "I'll get the other car started!"

"Come back here!" Cort yelled. "Stay under cover! I'll take care of that!"

THE PENTARIANS had come around now and were set for another sweep. As they bore in at treetop level, Butch yelled, "It's no good. The controls on this thing are jammed! We're not going anywhere!"

Cort, his eyes on the Pentarian car, jumped away from the Space Wagon and out onto open ground, hoping desperately to draw the green fire away from the exposed girl who was working desperately with the controls of the second car. "It's no use," she cried. "This one's dead, too!"

Cort's move was more successful than he'd hoped. The gunner upstairs had only a few seconds to direct his fire. Cort's move split his target, and the man couldn't make up his mind which sitting duck to pot. As a result, his fire swept in a line between Cort and Greta, touching neither of them. Cort raised two heat blisters on the airborne craft as it went by, but inflicted no great damage.

Now, Butch went into action. His plump face red from exertion, he pulled his cats from the useless car and ran to Greta who sat helplessly in the other craft. "Can you ride a horse?" he asked, and without waiting for an answer, seized the girl and flung her astride the back of one of the great cats. "Dig your hands into the fur and hang on," he wheezed. "Maggie's been rode before! Head for those rock hills over south! Wait for us there!"

He handed Greta the silver lead chains and gave a shrill whistle. "Get going, babies! Play-time! Big race! Take to the hills! Maggie! Mike! Scat!"

The cats had evidently done this sort of thing before and had enjoyed it. With no further urging, they started away on their twelve legs at a speed no race horse could have begun to equal—two black and orange streaks leveling out across the rough desert floor, with Greta hanging onto Maggie's back like grim death.

Butch turned immediately and fled toward the hull of the Space Wagon. Cort, his narrowed eyes on the slowly arcing Pentarian car, said, "Fast thinking, Butch. Good work! She may get a chance to live a little longer over in those rocks."

"What would you say our chances are?"

The crippled car had nosed around now for another attack. Cort poised his two guns. "Pretty slim. There'll probably be more of them flocking in soon. When they can come at us from two directions at once—we're through."

"You know something?" Butch moaned. "I should have stayed on Mars."

AS THE two Martian tigers kited toward the rock hills, Greta had time to think of nothing but hanging on. It was like riding a fur rug thrown over a varnished barrel. It seemed impossible to the girl that any animal's skin could slide around its body so loosely, and still remain attached to the bone and muscle underneath.

She was astride the giant cat at a point just back of the forward pair of legs. Maggie's hard shoulder bones, pumping like locomotive driving rods, kept slamming against Greta's thighs in a seemingly deliberate effort to unseat her. Desperately, Greta sought to slide rearward, but only to come perilously close to the claws of the cat's middle legs as they slashed along in deadly rhythm.

Several times, the girl was almost hurled to the rocky desert floor and to possible serious injury. But the long graceful strides of the great fanged Maggie was exceedingly smooth, and Greta gradually lost her fear of becoming unseated.

This swift retreat from danger was not to her liking, and she would have objected strenuously had she had the opportunity. But Butch's move was so quick and decisive, that Greta was flying across the desert on Maggie's back before she had time to collect her wits.

As the vast, rocky labyrinth ahead loomed larger, she entertained thoughts of reversing her direction and returning to the ship. She made some effort toward doing this, but Maggie entirely ignored the order to turn around.

Then, side by side, the giant cats swept in between two great boulders and began mounting the steep slopes toward the higher reaches of the jagged incline. Sudden panic swept through Greta. Were these beasts never going to stop? They gave no indication of it as they hurtled along sharp-edged ridges and leaped fifty-foot crevasses without breaking stride. Several times Greta closed her eyes as she sailed through space over death traps a thousand feet deep.

As the desert floor fell further and further below, Greta got the odd feeling that Mike and Maggie knew exactly where they were going, so direct was their course and so swift their pace. This she dismissed as foolishness, but the cats kept moving upward to reach, finally, what seemed to be the crest of the immense boulder pile, and to start down the other side.

NOW came the real panic. Beside this wild downward rush, the trip upward had been completely safe. Here was the sickening sensation of falling straight downward into nothingness. Several times, Greta was sure that Maggie had misjudged her leap and that she and the tiger were doomed to crash on the rocks hundreds of feet below. But each time, there was the soft breaking of the fall as the cat's huge pads gripped and held the ledges toward which she continually hurled her graceful body.

Then, the descent was over. The cats dropped into a level, rock-floored canyon and loped a quarter of a mile of its length before they turned abruptly through a narrow passage Greta would have overlooked entirely. Fifty yards of this and they trotted into a hidden paradise—a green gem of an oasis hidden in the heart of this vast rock pile.

There was thick, lush grass—green, but of a much darker shade than that of Earth and trees with dark graceful branches hanging into a crystal pool in which silver fish could be seen darting in and out among bright blue rocks below.

The two cats trotted straight to the pool and thrust their hot muzzles into the water—thus revealing to Greta that they had—in a sense—known where they were going. They'd smelled the water a long way off and had moved unerringly toward it.

Somewhat shaken by her experience, Greta dropped to the grass beside the pool and lay there, her head spinning, her heart thumping in her bosom. Maggie lapped at the water until she'd had her fill, then sat back on her haunches and yawned a great saber-toothed yawn. For a few moments, the Martian cat watched her mate who lay crouched over the edge of the pool striving to knock the silver fish out of the water with lightning-like sweeps of his huge paw.

Mike had no success at this, and his temper began to shorten with each successive miss. His throaty growls echoed and reechoed among the rocks.

Maggie lost interest in this diversion and turned her attention to Greta. With a grin that opened her mouth and made her throat appear as a great pink tunnel, she padded over to the girl and sought to lick her cheek. Maggie's tongue would certainly have ripped Greta's face wide open had it found its mark. But Greta pushed the cat away with a sharp command to lie down.

Maggie sat back on her haunches and regarded Greta wistfully. Then, at some signal from Mike, Maggie turned away and the two cats trotted off side by side.

In panic now at the sudden loneliness, Greta called, "Maggie—Mike! Come back. Kitty—kitty—kitty! Come back, Maggie!"

BUT THE cats refused to obey, and Greta realized they had gone off looking for dinner. She stopped calling and lay back with her eyes closed. Her mind was now filled with thoughts and anxieties concerning Cort and Butch. A reaction of weakness seized her, and she realized how deep had been her shock at seeing Sam French cut down ruthlessly by the green fire. A sickness came to her at the memory, and she strove sternly for self-control.

How were Cort and Butch faring, she wondered? Were they still alive, or had they, too, been killed by the vicious flame guns? Biting her lip, she prayed fervently that they'd escaped. Then she tried deliberately to force away all thoughts of fear. Of course they'd escaped. Then, a thought came entirely unbidden to her mind. They had escaped, and she would yet feel Cort's strong arms around her—feel her body close to his.

She opened her eyes, leaned down over the edge of the pool and drank from its clear waters. As she got to her feet, the cool depths of the pool looked singularly inviting. She glanced quickly around the jewel-like park, then began stripping off her clothing. The thought of a plunge into the cool waters of the pond was more than Greta could resist.

But she was not to have that plunge immediately. As she dropped the last wispy bit of intimate apparel and stood there, a naked brown nymph, there came a transition that left her breathless.

First, the change of Pentarian day into night; an almost instantaneous darkening of the heavens, as the sun shot down below the horizon beyond the rocks. It was, she thought, as though a giant had drawn a black cape across the sky.

But this was not the only thing that filled her with wonder. Simultaneous with the coming of darkness, the pool became a thing of dazzling beauty. From its depths, there shot up a myriad of rainbow lights—every color from pale violet to deep orange, with the more fiery colors predominating, until the pool was transformed into a glowing fire pit.

There was no darkness. One form of light had been substituted for another. With the sun gone, the gorgeous phosphorescence from the pool lit up the park like a corner of fairyland.

Greta had just time to catch her breath in stunned surprise—overcome by the sheer beauty of the change. Then she saw something else—something so hideous that at first her eyes did not believe what they beheld.

She screamed and jumped—arms flung wide—into the multicolored waters of the pool.

CHAPTER FIVE

"I WONDER what they're sore about?" Butch asked somewhat plaintively. "Here we are, not doing any harm, and they start trying to pot us. Is that Pentarian hospitality?"

The Pentarian space car, still without reinforcements, was continuing its dogged attack. It crossed over again, the forward gun spouting green fire. Cort pressed close to the hull of the Space Wagon as the flame sizzled by, and then threw two quick shots upward with his spectrum guns. He succeeded only in raising a pair of heat blisters on the thradium bottom of the car. "They're getting cagey," he growled. "It doesn't look as though we'll get any of them before help arrives."

A dark evil face peered downward as the car shot across. "Gawd!" Butch muttered. "That guy Korbo's got a face to scare strong-hearted men. A puss right out of a grade-A nightmare. How you coming with that space car?"

They had dragged one of the portable cars into the shelter of the big ship, and between attacks, Cort was working grimly with the mechanism. "If they'll only give us a little more time. It's this damn jet connection. It's bent so we don't get a direct drive."

"Well, bend the thing back, damn it! That ought to be simple."

"This tube is four percent thradium. Maybe you'd like a crack at it?"

Butch leaned forward, but Cort pushed him away and exerted strength against the bent tube until the veins stood out on his forehead. "I'm getting—it—now."

"For crisake lookout!"

Cort glanced upward and threw himself sideways just in time to avoid being smashed to bits by the green fire stream. But as the Pentarian ship passed over, he flung a defiant curse after it and went back to his work.

"I think I've got it," he said finally.

"It's about time," Butch grunted. "Let's get upstairs where we've got—Hey! What the hell! Who turned out the lights?"

Butch had been moving toward the space car in broad daylight. Only four short steps ago. But by the time he touched the rubber seat, he was in complete darkness. Thus came night on Pentar; like a drop-off into an inky pit.

"They don't seem to fuss around with twilight out here," Cort observed. "Come on! Roll your lard into this egg crate and let's get away. We can sneak underneath them and head for that rock pile over there. If Greta shows a light, we'll pick her up."

"And my cats, too."

"Never mind those damn tigers. There isn't room."

THE CAPSULE jet of the space car glowed brightly for a moment as the fuel caught. Then, the light car arose silently to glide away into the black sky. Cort crouched over the controls, while Butch rubbed his thick posterior where it had come in violent contact with the floor. He sat up gingerly and looked backward in the darkness. "Goodbye, Sam," he said softly. "It was nice knowing you."

"We'll chalk up a score for Sam before we're through," Cort said grimly. "We've got something else to do first."

Butch leaned over the bulging rubber side and stared downward into the darkness. "We ought to be pretty well over that rock pile now. And I don't see any lights."

"We know she's safe, anyhow. Nobody would bother her with those cats around. Looks as though we'll have to wait until daylight."

There was a moment of silence, then Butch's voice in which a note of uncertainty predominated: "Yeah. Oh, sure. She's safe with Maggie and Mike all right."

Cort's quick frown was hidden by the darkness. "You don't seem too confident. What's on your mind."

"Nothing. I was just thinking."

"Thinking what?"

"Those cats. They didn't get their supper."

"What in the devil's wrong with you? Haven't we got more important things to worry about than—"

"That could be pretty important."

"You mean—"

"I don't mean anything. That is—I'm not sure. They're as civilized as two Martian cats could be, and they like Greta. But they must be pretty hungry, and—"

"What!"

"I really don't think they'd get rough. But we'll keep our ears open, and be ready to go downstairs quick," Cort gritted his teeth in frustration. "Damn this darkness—this helplessness. If those cats—"

Two beams of light cut through the darkness. They converged in a cross-fire on the motionless space car, catching Cort and Butch squarely in their merciless glare. A voice came out of the night—a sharp, cold voice. "Make a move, and you'll not live ten seconds."

"Hold on!" Cort yelled, and kicked at the controls. The car shot out into the darkness. But a mocking laugh drifted through the air, and a stream of green fire materialized in front of the car across the prow.

CORT SWERVED just in time to miss it, and just in time also to move within range of the search light beams which had followed the car's path unerringly. Again the laughter, and the voice: "It's no use. I suggest you stop this nonsense before I lose my temper and have you cut to pieces."

"How the hell do they stay on our tail that way?" Butch marveled.

"It's simple. They're spotting us in ultra-violet. We've probably been covered from the beginning." Then, in a louder voice: "All right. We don't seem to have much chance. Come on in."

"That's better."

There was a period of tense silence while the light beams shortened, converging on the helpless space car, and two more cars appeared in the circle of light sent out from their spots. They were cars of ancient design, but had been well cared for and were in excellent shape.

One of them swung close, and a tall man posing in a garment that looked like a magician's cape, called out an order: "Settle to the ground immediately or we'll blast you!"

"We don't know what we're standing over," Cort objected. "It may be dangerous."

"Not as dangerous as remaining aloft. Drop down."

Cort lowered the car slowly until it settled on even ground some twenty feet below. The other two cars dropped to either side, and a squad of tall, hard-faced men came into range of the spot lights.

"That one barking the orders is Korbo," Butch said in a low voice. "He's the one Greta pointed out."

"Get ready to jump for it," Cort whispered. "When they ask for our guns, give it to them from the hip—then run."

But Korbo had a remarkable pair of ears, or he was an excellent judge of men. He snapped, "Drop your harnesses—and be careful about it. Touch those guns, and you'll never know what hit you."

Cursing under his breath, Cort did as he was ordered, and saw Butch's harness drop to the ground beside his own.

"That's better," Korbo approved.

AT THIS instant, the tall Pentarian was pushed casually aside by a small, sparrow-like individual with a jutting nose, a mustache, and an air of genial authority. He was rolling a long black cigar from one corner of his mouth to the other, and he looked for all the world like a ward heeler from some large Earth city in the process of getting out the vote.

His voice was as hearty as his manner: "Well, now, if this isn't a pleasant surprise. A couple of boys from my old stomping ground. A couple of Earthmen for sure. How are things on the old ball of mud, anyhow?"

"Who the hell are you?" Butch asked bluntly.

The little man laughed. "Don't tell me you never heard of Boss Hagerty. Why, young feller, this is my territory out here. You're on Boss Hagerty's planet, son, and don't ever forget it. I'm the big wheel around here—the prize toad. I'm surprised, your not knowing that."

Hagerty pushed an open hand toward Cort, but the latter ignored it. "In that case, maybe you can answer a few questions," Cort said, making no attempt to keep the hostility from his voice.

Hagerty dropped his hand, but remained genial. "Sure thing, son. Ask away. Always like to put people straight."

"Why were we attacked by your ship without being given an opportunity to identify ourselves? Why was one of our men killed in cold blood by your murderers?"

"All a mistake, son. A big mistake. Sorry as hell it happened, but you got one of my boys, so that evens it up."

Butch's face went tight with rage. "Maybe that's what you think, shrimp, but—"

Boss Hagerty's smile remained warm and cordial as he motioned toward the closest uniformed underling. "You better give this lad the clouts," he laughed.

The tall soldier moved forward like a striking snake. His fist lashed out and Butch went sprawling to the ground. Cort leaped forward, but only to feel two of the deadly green-fire guns poked into his belly.

Little lines of mirth appeared at the corners of Hagerty's eyes. "Never did like to be called shrimp," he explained in a confidential voice. "I had to leave Earth on account of being called a name. A poll watcher on the West Side in Chicago accused me of being a crook, so I let him have it with a blackjack. I split his skull and he never woke up so I had to breeze. By the way, how *are* things in Chicago these days?"

Butch was back on his feet, rubbing his jaw and eyeing the jaunty little man with a look of bewilderment and disbelief. Hagerty smiled at him, grasped his pudgy hand and shook it cordially. "You boys are like a breath of spring. No fooling. Sorry my gang took out after you, but as I said, it was just one of those things. You came in without identifying yourselves, so how were they to know?"

"We brought in a load of heavy salt on the Space Wagon, and we had a crackup," Cort said. "There was no chance to—"

Hagerty waved his cigar airily. "Yeah. I know all about that. Thanks a lot. The salt's been unloaded and it's on its way to Hagerty City now." His grin deepened and his chest bulged out. "Get that? I even got a town named after me. I wish the boys in Chicago could know about it."

"They do," Cort retorted. "The whole solar system knows about Hagerty's Planet..."

CHAPTER SIX

THE LITTLE man looked honestly startled, then grinned from ear to ear. "No fooling? Well what do you know about that..." He looked as though he'd just been presented with a token of all mankind's admiration, and Cort marveled. If this cocky little upstart's pleasure was not genuine, then he was an amazingly good actor.

"Of course, I had to have some ability," Hagerty said confidentially, "but I got the breaks, too. This oversized ping pong ball was ripe to be knocked over. I passed up nine worlds after I ran out on that rap in Chicago, and finally stumbled on this place. Lots of plain luck involved."

Butch had been staring at Boss Hagerty with his mouth hanging open. Slowly, the bewildered man turned his eyes on Cort. "Is this guy for real?" he muttered.

Hagerty's happy smile did not change, but Cort saw his hand start to move as though to order another helping of the clouts for Butch.

In order to forestall this, Cort spoke swiftly concerning the first thing that came to his mind. "Hagerty—that's an Irish name. But you don't appear to be Irish."

Hagerty's mind was diverted. He grinned even deeper and set his teeth into the cigar. "I ain't," he admitted. "I'm a mongrel. A mixture of eighteen different breeds. That's where I get my ability. Now, a thoroughbred ain't got what I got, son. It takes a mongrel to step out and be at home in any company."

"I'm sure it does, and no doubt you've done very well for yourself, but—"

Hagerty turned now and waved a casual hand toward Korbo who had been sulking back in the shadows. "Forgot to introduce you to my Number One boy—Korbo here. Step up, Mac, and meet two boys from Earth."

Korbo came forward. He obeyed Hagerty's order swiftly, but made no effort to hide the sullenness and resentment in his face. Hagerty regarded him affectionately, slapped him on the arm and said, "I found Mac had a lot of hidden talents that only wanted developing. I picked him up and trained him, and now he's my hatchetman—my bully boy. Does all the dirty work and likes it. He's some punkins now, and he owes it all to me. Don't you, Mac?"

The evil-eyed Pentarian answered up promptly, "Yes, Master, I owe it all to you."

Hagerty grinned confidentially at Cort and made a deprecating gesture. "That Master stuff—it's their own idea. I tried to discourage it, but what can you do?" He shrugged expressively. "It comes of their own free will and from genuine love, so I let it pass."

CORT OPENED his mouth to comment, but the mercurial mind of Boss Hagerty had leap-frogged to another subject, and his tongue was quicker. "By the way—the boys told me you got a menagerie with you. From the way they talked, it sounded like a couple of Martian cats. They had some wild story about a girl riding one of them up into the rocks. Kind of sounds like my boys have been smoking the wrong weed—right?"

Cort had to make a swift decision. He made it and said, "You're right—the wrong weed."

Boss Hagerty seemed disappointed. "Then that little dark-headed gal didn't come back with you, eh? I was kind of hoping she would. These Pentarian females are pretty unappetizing. They're big as horses and usually just as ugly..." He nodded toward the tall, silent squadron "...or short and squat and hairless as cucumbers. There's only two kinds out here."

To Cort, this seemed an opportune time to press a possible advantage. He said, "No, she didn't come. But she told us about the agreement Korbo made concerning her father and one more load of salt. So we brought the ransom, and of course you'll produce John Lansing."

Hagerty rocked back on his heels, squinted speculatively at a spot over Cort's head, and said, "Boy, you make it sound pretty tough talking about ransom that way. You make old Boss Hagerty sound like a hard article. But if you knew how bad we needed that salt..."

"I'm not criticizing," Cort replied. "I'm just establishing my identity, proving I'm an authorized agent for Greta Lansing."

"Uh-huh." Hagerty drew deeply on his cigar. "Nice name that—Greta Lansing. Sure wish she'd have come along with you. Wish I could turn her dad over to you, too, but I can't do it. The damned old fool ran away."

"Ran away—"

"That's what I said. Had him bedded down all nice and comfy out on one of Korbo's farms, and he didn't appreciate the hospitality. Maybe he'll turn up, though. Let's hope so..."

Hagerty turned abruptly back toward the space car in which he'd ridden. He motioned toward Cort and Butch with a jerk of his head. "But let's not stand here gassing all night. Me—I got a little lake resort up in them rocks—a place I come to relax when the affairs of state get heavy. You boys might as well come along and get something to eat. Then we'll talk a few things over. Believe it or not, I could use a couple of able bodied brains to help run this cockeyed little world of mine. We'll talk it over." He beckoned with his cigar. "Come on and ride with me. Korbo'll see to bringing your crate along." As he waited, Hagerty ran a speculative eye over the trim Earth car. "Nice little boat. Glad we didn't have to cut it up."

CORT'S EMOTIONS were mixed as he sat beside the silent Butch in Hagerty's car. The pilot had never run into anything like Hagerty, and he was somewhat at a loss. Finding the little opportunist far out here on Pentar, was like tripping over a Venusian monkeyman entering the Biltmore in white tie and tails; a trifle out of place, to say the least.

But Cort was content to give Hagerty only half his mind. The rest was occupied with wondering about Greta. His instinct had told him to lie about her presence on Pentar, and Hagerty's subsequent remarks had proven his instinct correct. But there was the problem of where Greta had gone, how he was going to contact her, and how they were going to find her father and quit the planet. Possibly the Space Wagon would limp back to the solar system, but if so, how were they going to get their hands on it? Cort did not even hope that Boss Hagerty would send them off with his blessing. He knew that so far as Hagerty was concerned, they were on Pentar for the balance of their lives. The only question was how long those lives would last.

Conundrums of this sort were threshing through Cort's mind when he caught sight of the strange glow off in the darkness. He watched this brighten and increase in size and intensity as the ship swept toward it. Now, the multi-colored lights of the glow deepened and took on movements like some warm aurora borealis, or a tremendous display of fireworks.

Then, the ships breasted a dark ridge, and there lay below them a small, cuplike park drenched with various and beautiful shades of coloring which seemed to emanate from a gigantic fire in its center.

Boss Hagerty chuckled, taking personal satisfaction from the amazement of the two men. "A little place I ran onto," he said modestly. "There's something funny in the lake down there; some kind of phosphorus. It lights up the whole layout like a Christmas tree on Broadway. The pond is right for swimming, and there's grass and trees and everything. You'll really go for it."

The space cars settled noiselessly upon the thick sod of the lawn, and Hagerty led the way to the flaming lake. "The boys'll bring the grub from the cars," he stated, "and we'll have ourselves a spread. A few drinks won't go bad, either—"

Hagerty stopped talking abruptly as his eyes followed those of Butch who was staring at something on the bank of the pond. Cort also was looking down in tense silence. He glanced swiftly at Butch as Boss Hagerty stepped forward and bent over.

"Hmmm," Hagerty muttered, "what have we here now? As I live and breathe! A pair of panties—girl's panties—and a brassiere and stockings for a pair of nice long legs. All the rest of it, too. Everything a girl'd wear, but no babe to fill 'em. What do you know about that?"

He turned to Cort and Butch. There was a smile on his face; a smile of hurt sensibilities; the look of a man who had been treated badly. When he spoke, his voice was gently reproachful. He said, "Boys, you'd better give these two chaps the treatment. I'm afraid they've got some lumps coming on account of they tried to bamboozle old Hagerty. Telling him that dark-haired armful was way back on Earth, when she's really wandering around here somewhere as naked as a jay-bird. Yeah, these sons've got some lumps coming."

Butch went down with a moan from a swift murderous blow from the closest Pentarian. Cort was more alert. He stepped inside of the first blow aimed at him and sank his fist up to the wrist on an untightened belly. This brought a jaw down within reach. He hit the jaw and almost tore the attached head off. This being no time for sportsmanship, he kicked the next comer in the groin with enough force to numb his own foot. The man screamed and doubled up. Cort's knee smashed his nose into a blood-spouting pulp, and there were two down.

But there were too many to go, and Cort was swiftly smothered under an avalanche of murderous blows. His whole body became the home of various and agonizing pains.

Then, as he went down and out, he heard Boss Hagerty's softly complaining voice: "Can you imagine them trying to get cozy with a good guy like me?"

CHAPTER SEVEN

MAGGIE HAD grown exceedingly fond of the dark slim she-human—almost as much so as of the fat, greasy he-human she had learned to know as her master. Mike, however, was her true lord, and allegiance to him came first. He was pretty much neutral so far as all humans were concerned. He'd learned not to eat the ones he knew intimately—at least, he had never been hungry enough in their presence to give it serious thought—and he somewhat grudgingly obeyed the commands of the fat he-human who provided nourishment at the proper times. Also, he had nothing against the dark she for whom his silly mate had formed such an attachment. But he would put up with no foolishness, so after the dark she-human had been brought to the water, he signaled Maggie that it was time to forage for food.

Both cats were thoroughly aware of the many humans hiding in the neighborhood of the clear water. The humans had not been seen, even by the sharp eyes of the Martian tigers, but the scent was so heavy, the cats could have run without hesitation from one hiding place to the next.

Probably a pair of lazy cats would have dined sumptuously without traveling more than ten steps, but Maggie and Mike were not lazy, and were willing to exert a little effort in order to find non-human food.

Side by side, their twelve legs moving in almost perfect rhythm, they went up the rocky slopes as they had come until the faint scent of meat was registered in Mike's sharp nostrils. He swung to the right, Maggie still dutifully by his side, and lunged straight toward a peculiar red bush, the like of which he'd never seen. One sweep of his huge right front paw tore the bush up by the roots and revealed a small, terrorized rodent with a heavy musky odor.

Mike slapped a paw down on the creature and had the annoyance of feeling the fragment of meat stick between two of his toes. He growled and pried it out with the end of his two-foot right fang. This operation completed, there was not enough left to eat, so he pushed the dead rodent contemptuously toward Maggie. Maggie licked it up daintily with her great platter of a tongue and got the morsel caught most unfortunately between two of her teeth.

Maggie snarled her frustration, and the two cats loped on through the rocks, entering into a telepathic agreement to waste no more time on tidbits too small to chew on.

Larger game, however, was so scarce as to be practically nonexistent. Beyond the rocks, they came upon some sort of a desert serpent. It was many yards long and was viciously fanged. Upon sight of Mike and Maggie, it coiled itself into a scaly heap, reared its head high, and prepared to meet any attack.

INSTINCTIVELY, the cats knew a bite from this reptile would mean certain death. Nonetheless, they went after it with cunning and dispatch. Putting themselves at opposite points of a circle, they danced daintily around the hideous snake until bewilderment shone in its cruel little eyes. In so doing, they were in a position so that the snake could face but one of them. It chose Mike, so Maggie, at just the right moment, leaped in with the speed of black and orange light to smash the flat bone of the creature's skull.

They sat down then, side by side on their haunches, and watched the thing thresh violently in its death struggle. When the worst was over, they stretched the long body out and squatted down to dinner.

But again they were confounded. This reptile was composed entirely of rubber, or some other material equally as resistant and unappetizing. For a long time, they ground down patiently upon the snake carcass—gnawed until their massive jaws were aching from weariness. And, yet, they had hardly made an abrasion on the scaly surface.

They gave up simultaneously and in complete disgust. Raging at the time wasted, Mike went into a snarling frenzy and began clawing a great hole in the ground. The hole large enough to suit him, he pushed the snake therein and clawed fresh earth over it until it was completely buried. Somewhat mollified by this vengeance, but still mighty hungry, the two cats went off again at a tireless lope.

Some ten miles away, they spent a good ten minutes carefully stalking a gigantic bird that promised much nourishment. But the foul awakened at the crucial moment and plunged with a terrified scream into the air. Mike lunged upward after it, describing a great arc that was forty feet from the ground at its highest point. He came down with a mouthful of feathers and a rage burning as fiercely as a blast furnace.

Maybe they could have done very well on Mars, but on Pentar, it seemed, Mike and Maggie were complete busts as hunters.

It was now that Mike began wondering what he was doing out here in the desert. Why waste time in this fashion when he knew a place where the human-smell was so heavy, it made one drool? Without further thought, he reversed his route and went back as he had come, the ever-faithful Maggie by his side.

As they went up the outside of the immense rock pile, night descended upon Pentar in the twinkling of an eye. But the cats gave no thought whatever to this phenomenon. They were not concerned in the least as to how night either came or went. It did not inconvenience them one iota, because they could see equally well at midnight or high noon.

BUT THEY were annoyed a great deal when they discovered a change in conditions at the now brilliantly-lighted park. Only a short time ago, the human-smell had been heavy enough to bite. Now it was faint, telling them the humans had gone elsewhere. In a rage now, from gnawing hunger, they began to work independently, sniffing carefully through the smell-trails, trying to unravel at least one and follow it where ever it might lead.

But again and again the trails led them up against solid rock at the far end of the park. Again and again they started over, only to be brought up repeatedly against the same hard barrier, until finally Mike hurled himself, raging, at the perpendicular cliff and got knocked backward thirty feet for his pains.

He returned again to the wall, to find Maggie sniffing at a small opening the weight of his huge body had caused to occur. Mike pushed her roughly aside, applied his own nose to the opening, and was rewarded by a human-smell so rich as to make his jowls quiver.

While Maggie snarled with impatience, Mike attacked the opening with fang and claw. His great saber tusks drew sparks from the rocks, and his ten-inch claws jerked out boulders by the roots. Gradually, the opening increased until Mike could force his body through it without losing too much skin. Maggie followed behind him, her six legs straining to force the rest of her along under the low ledge that continued inward while the human-smell increased to such a point as to be almost palatable.

After a seemingly endless trip with the roof forcing them to scrape their bellies continuously against the stone floor, the cats came at last to a place where they looked down into a sizeable room from a place just under the ceiling.

At the far end of the room, two great flares burned mournfully from clefts in the rocks, throwing great dancing shadows on the walls. Between the flares were a series of stone steps leading up to what was obviously an altar. Before this altar stood a squat, ugly, naked man who was obviously engaged in some act of worship. He was holding aloft in both hands a great swatch of what both cats knew to be long, dark hair.

As a matter of fact, the hair made Maggie stir with a sudden sense of indefinable disloyalty. It made Mike remember the dark-haired she-human—remember her with gustatory relish and with longing.

But their main attention was centered upon the man. They knew nothing of altars, of worship, or of strange sacrifices. They knew only one thing. Here at last was supper.

And about time, too.

CHAPTER EIGHT

GRETA, when standing unclothed there by the fabulous fire-pool, had been completely occupied by the rapturous riot of color. Her ears were oblivious of even ordinary sounds, so she certainly did not hear the stealthy approach of softly whispering feet.

The horror of it hit her in one sickening second when, from the corner of her eye, she caught movement and turned her head to see the ugly, entirely hairless little man creeping silently toward her.

And he was only one of many. Seemingly materialized from vapor, they were all around her, crouching, waiting, leering in lascivious eagerness at her perfect body.

Greta screamed and leaped into the center of the pool as the little man jumped toward her with arms spread wide. She sank down into the stillness of the waters, and immediately all was calm and restful. There in the heart of the flaming pond, she thought it must indeed have been a hallucination.

But a rough hand was entwined in her hair and she was dragged to the surface. It was no dream. It had been stark reality, and she was being hauled ashore by a grinning little monster, while dozens of the creatures danced about on the shore and chanted some foul gibberish Greta couldn't understand.

The girl fought valiantly, but it availed her nothing. The man was entirely at home in the water, and there were countless willing hands waiting to drag Greta, in her nakedness and shame, to the pond bank.

Four of the creatures grasped her in such a way as to render her completely helpless. She could only writhe like some beautiful mermaid brought from the deep onto dry land.

It was then that she heard—or thought she heard—a few starkly Earthian words salted into the gibberish. She could have sworn one of the creatures howled: "Some dame! Some dame." That another mouthed a familiar phrase: "I'll be double-damned." But Greta had a feeling the words meant little to the speakers.

In desperation, she added her own voice to the din: "Please! Please let me go! At least, let me have my clothes! Why do you treat me this way?"

The captors paid no attention to their prisoner's pleadings. They continued to howl in glee, and Greta noted that several kept glancing fearfully up toward the sky and urging the others on a course toward the far end of the park. The movement in that direction became a procession with Greta's bearers leading the way and the rest of the obscene little creatures following close behind.

THE GIRL was carried directly to the face of a perpendicular wall and wondered, in panic, if they intended to dash her brains out against its stone surface. But once there, a group of them flung their combined weight against the wall and a totally invisible door swung slowly open.

This revealed a flare-lit passage leading straight into the cliff. Carrying Greta triumphantly, holding her high over their heads, Greta's captors led the babbling procession down the corridor and into a vast room carved out of solid rock.

In the center of this room was a raised block into which light chains were bolted. These chains were attached to anklets with which the little men speedily imprisoned Greta as on an auction block, where every eye in the place could feast upon her beauty.

The girl stood there with her head hanging in utter shame, discouragement and hopelessness. She had come to the end. Of her exact fate, she was ignorant, but now it mattered little. She hoped it would be quick death of some sort. That at least was preferable to torture, or her becoming the feature of some ghastly act of obscenity with thousands of lustful eyes witnessing her final degradation.

The assembled savages were in no hurry to proceed with the program, whatever it was to be. They kept up the weird, mournful chant they had begun by the pool, and were now forming a snake dance about the stone platform as they pressed in closer and closer to their lovely captive. As the line swayed in an uneven circle, some of them grew bolder and darted in to pass their hands, almost in reverence, through Greta's long, shining hair.

Then, one facet of this nightmare dawned on the girl. These people were entirely hairless. Not so much as the finest down was visible upon their shiny bullet heads and squat bodies. And their actions indicated it was Greta's hair that attracted them, sent them into this ecstatic frenzy.

The stricken girl shuddered as she felt the hands brushing against the hair that swept in glory down her back and touched her shapely ankles. She had been standing with head bowed and eyes closed. Now, she opened her eyes to see the ugly face of a wizened little female grimacing up at her. The woman's lips moved to reveal twisted teeth. Her voice was a croak, but was intelligible: "I talk like you," the woman said.

"Then help me—please help me."

"I listen to Boss—to Boss Hagerty. I learn. You talk like him. I talk like him."

"What do you want with me?"

The woman frowned importantly. "Hair. If gods want—we give you to gods—with knife."

"How—do you find out if the gods want me?"

"The god-man. He find out. He take that." The woman pointed to Greta's hair. "He go in to gods. Ask them. Over there."

She pointed to a closed stone panel before which, even now, a wizened little man was kneeling. A man who had taken no part in the frenzy, but had remained alone in his meditations.

AT THIS POINT, he arose, turned and approached the platform. Instantly, all activity stopped and he passed among the still creatures to mount the stone beside Greta. She could see him closely now, and noted his eyes seemed unseeing, but were filled with an odd ecstasy of their own; an entranced look as though he communed with unseen forces. From a thin belt around his waist—his sole stitch of wearing apparel—he took a short-bladed knife and grasped Greta's hair at the nape of her neck. With a few swift strokes, he cut it completely away.

A soft cry went up from the watching throngs, as though this act had given them some sort of emotional release.

Ignoring everyone, the man went down from the platform carrying the hair in both hands as one would carry an offering. He walked straight to the door from whence he'd come, and now it had been opened by men inching along on their knees. Evidently it was a holy door before which no man stood erect.

The bearer of Greta's dark locks went inside, after which the door was closed again.

Now, everyone waited in silence.

The mood had changed into one of silent respect, almost of gloom, and Greta whispered to the crone who was still at her feet, "And what if the gods don't want me?"

The woman shrugged. "Then some man take you. The strongest man," she added, as she got up and wandered away.

The dead silence was oppressing. The tension of waiting was unbearable to the terrified girl. Why didn't they get it over with? Why did they torture her with this ghastly waiting? Why didn't the gods decide one way or another?

Then it seemed the gods were displeased because, from beyond the stone door, there came sounds of savage distemper; sounds that petrified the hairless people who made it obvious this was something entirely new; sounds their gods had never made before.

But to Greta, they were easily identifiable. She had heard them before and, in a flash, came understanding. Somehow, Maggie and Mike had come back from hunting and found their way into the place beyond that door. And they had not fared well on their hunting trip, because the savage roars and snarls were those of famished Martian tigers. No other sound in all creation was quite so blood-chilling and hideous.

With this new knowledge, there came to Greta a fantastic plan for her own salvation. A plan which, if it succeeded, would do so because of its very audacity.

REACHING down, she snapped the anklets from her legs and held out her arms for attention. "Listen to me—all of you. I have tolerated this out of curiosity, but now I grow weary of it. I am a goddess. The Goddess Greta, far stronger than your own gods to which you pray."

She waited until the few who understood her translated the words into the jargon these people used. As a muttering of anger went up, she continued, "Far stronger than your gods, and I have come to rule over you. As proof of my power, I have caused your priest to be destroyed, as he prayed to your weak gods and they were powerless to protect him. Even now he has disappeared, and two of my creatures occupy your sacred room. Throw open the door and let them out, or I will smash it to bits with my magic! Throw it open, I say!"

When the meaning reached the kneeling men, they went into a hurried and fearful conference, after which they crawled forward on their knees and drew back the panel.

Greta called out with far more confidence than she felt: "Maggie! Mike! Come out here. Come to me this minute."

In the doorway stood the two great Martian tigers. Well-fed and only lazily interested. Maggie was purring out her satisfaction over a full stomach. She opened her mouth and grinned a great grin at all who cared to look. Then, recognizing Greta, mainly from scent, the cat trotted toward the platform.

Mike stood motionless for a few moments. Then, because he had nothing better to do, he followed his mate to sit back on his haunches beside her and in front of Greta.

"Look in your sacred room, I say," Greta called out. "See if your holy man has not vanished."

A few of the braver ones complied, to come forth almost immediately and fall on their faces in terror at this new goddess and her terrible creatures. Soon, every face in the room except those of Greta, Maggie, and Mike, were pressed to the floor.

"Bring me my clothes by the pool," Greta commanded, and many of the people hastened to obey.

The girl sighed deeply in sudden relief. She had won through—turned defeat to victory in a few brief moments.

Maybe I lost my shirt, she told herself, but I certainly ended up the top goddess of this outfit!

CHAPTER NINE

BUT CORT and Butch had not fared nearly so well as their lovely and quick-thinking companion of the space voyage. After the episode at the flame pool, there was a long nightmare-time of unconsciousness and half-consciousness resulting from the vicious, cold-blooded attack of Boss Hagerty's muscle men.

When Cort came to, his first impression was of a terrible odor; a fetid reek that violated his nostrils and brought him to the point of retching.

He opened his eyes to a dim half-light and made out the still form of Butch lying beside him on a dirt floor. He nudged him and was rewarded by a stirring of the fat body. Cort said, "Wake up, Lard. Looks like somebody brought us home."

"Don't call me Lard," Butch muttered, then groaned as he sought to struggle erect. "Good lord! What the hell happened?"

"We got worked over. Boss Hagerty's boys—remember?"

"Remember? My shoulder. My leg. I think they're both busted."

"We're probably lucky to be alive. I wonder if they got Greta?"

"Not unless they got Mike and Maggie too."

"But what could have happened to her? Her clothes were lying on the bank of that pond."

Butch had come to a sitting position. He was gingerly patting an egg-sized lump under his right ear. "Say—that pool was the damndest thing I ever saw."

"Lord knows how she and the cats got there."

"Either someone stripped her—and I don't think they did because the clothes were in too neat a pile—or she went for a swim."

"And didn't come up again?"

"Could be. Maybe there was something funny about that water hole. Maybe Greta was drowned."

Cort had been holding his head in his hands. He raised his head and there was frustration—misery—in the one eye that was still open. The other eye showed nothing but a large purple swelling. "We've got to find out. I've got to know!"

"Well," Butch filled in with more cheer, "we know it wasn't Maggie or Mike. When they eat people, they don't stop to undress them. Their dinner goes down shoes and all." Butch frowned and turned somber. "What I'd like to know is where those cats went."

"What I'd like to know is where the hell we are."

Cort got to his feet and began examining the place. He found it to be about ten feet square and built of solid stone. The ceiling, also of rock, was about ten feet up, and only one small window aired the foul place. There were no furnishings; nothing to sit on except a boulder in one corner.

BUTCH STRUGGLED to his feet, swayed dizzily and staggered to the boulder. He sat down on it and groaned anew. "Wherever this trap is, I hope we aren't in it for good. Maybe they plan to leave us here. Then we'd starve!"

"It doesn't seem logical," Cort said, "but maybe—"

His words were broken off by a startled yelp from Butch, and Cort turned to see the fat man sprawled on the dirt floor. "That damn rock," Butch yelled. "It moved!"

As the two men stared, the boulder sifted in its setting, and one edge of it lifted a few inches. From the crack underneath, caused by this lifting, there came a harsh whisper: "Give me a hand, will you?"

Both men jumped to comply. By exerting their joint efforts against one side of the boulder, they were able to lift it high enough so that a thin, almost naked creature found clearance and slithered from beneath it. "Thanks," the creature said. "I couldn't have made it alone."

The man was completely exhausted from his efforts. He dropped to the floor and sat propped half-erect against the wall of the prison. Both Butch and Cort stared at him, and for a few moments they were both speechless.

The man looked ready to expire from malnutrition and abuse. He had once been a big man, but now he was little more than bones and a hideously mottled skin. His beard was thick and matted and would have made an excellent home for a nest of mice, if indeed the mice had not already taken up residence. His eyes were watery and red rimmed but, in spite of all this, he managed a weak smile.

"Welcome to the Vanderbilt, boys. The room service leaves something to be desired, but you'll get used to it. Who are you, and where did you come from?"

"Who the hell are you?" Butch retorted.

The man laughed weakly. "The name is John, John Lansing—or at least that's what it was. I don't recognize myself anymore, but that's who I was. John Lansing— gentleman at large—space adventurer—pilot second to none—nonconformist in all things except good liquor.

You wouldn't happen to have a flask in your pocket, would you?"

"Greta's old man!" Butch mouthed in wonder.

THE WORDS brought a rapid change in the man. He came to his feet and leaped toward Cort who was nearest him. "What was that? Greta! My daughter—you know her? She came back to this accursed planet? Speak, damn it! Tell me..."

Cort took Lansing by his scrawny arms and eased him down on the boulder. "Take it easy, mister. You're about done in. I'll tell you all about it."

"Then tell me. What're you waiting for?"

"My name is Liggett—Cort Liggett. This is Xerxes Mecropoulis...we call him Butch for short. Your daughter contacted me on Mars and talked me into bringing a load of heavy salt to Pentar, which was to be used to gain your freedom."

The old man groaned. "The little fool! She should have known Hagerty wouldn't keep his word. He'll take her and— Where is she now? What happened to her?"

"We don't know. Korbo attacked us after we made a crash landing—and it looked bad—"

"So I put her on a tiger and sent her into some rocks," Butch chimed in.

Lansing's eyes narrowed. He tightened visibly. Then wilted and mirrored utter defeat. When he spoke, it was to no one in particular—merely a statement of complete frustration: "I'd had a little hope up to now. It's amazing how long hope lives. How it refuses to die." He raised his eyes to Cort. "When they brought you in, I thought maybe this was it—the break. But I should have known by looking at you. Two men beaten silly by Hagerty's bully boys. What else could I expect, really."

"You're all wrong, old timer," Butch said. "We got our lumps, but we aren't nuts. You see, I own a couple of Martian cats, which we brought along. They're house broken to a certain extent. Wouldn't eat humans or anything like that—"

"You mean those six-legged monstrosities from the Martian hills?

"That's right."

"How do you know they wouldn't eat a human? No one ever tamed a Martian tiger."

Cort held up a hand. "This is getting us nowhere," he said sharply. "The situation is this: Lansing, Hagerty, and his men took us and we went to a strange lake that seemed to be full of fire—"

"The Flame Pool," Lansing said impatiently. "Hagerty uses it for outings, and there's something else there, too. But go on."

"Greta must have been there before us, because we found her clothes on the bank, as though she'd gone in for a swim. But that's all. Greta wasn't there, nor were the cats."

"Then we got our lumps and landed in this brig," Butch said.

"So, while we don't know where Greta is, we know Hagerty or Korbo didn't have her—at least not at that time."

"You said there was something else at that pool," Butch cut in. "What did you mean?"

"The Hairless Ones. They have an outlet at the pool—a temple."

"There's an awful lot about this planet we don't know," Butch retorted. "Maybe you'd better brief us."

"Give it from the beginning. If anything's to be done, we've got to have some idea of the score."

"It's Hagerty," Lansing said, "all Hagerty. You see, from time immemorial, this has been a planet of warfare between the Big Ones and the Hairless Ones, with the latter staying pretty much in the saddle. They've killed each other and lived only to fight and die, but neither side ever won a victory of annihilation. But neither side developed, either. They had no time for research and education, what with the rigors of staying alive. It was just a backward planet where death was the nature of things.

"Then Hagerty came along. This rotten little opportunist from Earth was running away from a murder charge, when he came to Pentar and sensed his opportunity. He's a genius of sorts, and with his political experience, he checked the situation and threw in with the Big Ones. Took them over, rather, and showed them how to hammer the Hairless Ones into submission. On the strength of this, he took over the planet for himself—"

CORT FROWNED and broke in: "You said they are backward here. Yet, we were attacked by men in space cars—"

"The cars—the guns—everything modern, was imported from other worlds by Hagerty. Now, he's started manufacturing on a slave labor basis, using the Hairless Ones as slaves. That's why the heavy salt is so important to him. It's needed in his manufacturing plants. They can hardly function without it."

"Quite a boy, this Hagerty," Butch commented.

"Also utterly dishonest and entirely ruthless."

"So we've discovered—especially the ruthless part."

"Another thing he lacks here on Pentar is desirable women. The females here leave much to be desired. He overcame this by importing—kidnapping—girls from Earth and Venus. But there were two drawbacks to this:

Those he procured were worn out and destroyed quickly by the insatiable lust of the Big Ones, and Hagerty is smart enough to know he can't go out for kidnapping in a big way. The solar planets let him alone because he's so far away, but they could come out and smash him if the stench got too strong. So he sits here on his world and yearns for beautiful women."

"Like Greta," Butch said, and drew a scowl from Cort.

"Keep your big trap shut!"

But Lansing reacted only through weariness. "It's all right. Indignation is a luxury for which I no longer have the strength. One becomes realistic in a place like this. Yes—beautiful girls like Greta."

"You haven't told us where we are."

"In Korbo's Processing Plant Number Two. We grind rock here for the new roads Hagerty is building."

"You said Hagerty helped the Big Ones beat the Hairless Ones. Are they completely subjugated?"

"Not entirely as yet, but it's only a question of time. They've gone underground where they're hard to get at, but Korbo corralled plenty of them. They're held in captivity and fed into the factories where they are systematically killed from starvation and over-work. It's a calculated process of eliminating the race."

"You're working in this factory also?"

"Yes, and you two are here for that purpose too, no doubt. We'll die faster than normal because we have the hatred of the Hairless Ones to contend with. We're of

Hagerty's race, and it's a little like being in a prison where the other convicts are down on you—only here it's worse. The Hairless Ones have more talent for slow torture than any prison full of convicts."

John Lansing got up from the boulder. "I've got to go back now. The other end of this tunnel leads through my cell, and they mustn't find out I'm gone. My two-hour rest period is about over, so I'll probably see you in the factory. Will you help me with this stone?"

They raised the boulder, and John Lansing left as he had come. "Buck up, old pal," Butch said in parting. "Things'll work out. Anybody figures they're going to cut my rations better think again."

Lansing vanished into the tunnel. The stone was dropped back into place and the two men sat staring at the wall.

"Well," Butch sighed, "at least we know the score."

"That we do. Now, I'm wondering what happened to Greta."

CHAPTER TEN

HER COUP having succeeded, Greta realized the time had come for some good constructive thinking and planning. She sat on the stone platform decently clothed again and with her back against Maggie's satiny shoulder.

Around her, the Hairless Ones continued to remain as they were, faces pressed to the floor. Greta, working from minute to minute, sensed an opportunity here to completely grasp the reins of the situation. It seemed the next logical step. But, with the time for decision and action having arrived, she found it wasn't so easy. She was ready to do something, but what?

With these thoughts mulling through her mind, she noted the complete passivity of the Hairless Ones. Were they trying to graft their noses to the floor? Why didn't they get up and go about their business?

Then, she realized they were waiting for her. They were hers, but she didn't know what to do with them. At least, she told herself, she could have a little privacy. With this in mind, she got to her feet, assumed the stance she felt a goddess would assume, and pointed imperiously toward the exit door. "Go!" she commanded. "Get hence! Scram! Beat it! Your goddess would be alone."

That sounds silly, she thought to herself. But evidently it did not sound so to the Hairless Ones because, after the necessary translations were made, they began crawling toward the door. This manner of exit interested Maggie a great deal. She snapped her tail and snarled her appreciation of the grotesque exodus. And her snarls helped speed it up, until not a Hairless One remained in the room.

Alone now with the cats, Greta did some heavy thinking. She yearned above all for knowledge of what had happened to Cort and Butch. Had they been killed by the green fire at the spaceship? Probably they had, she thought, and the sickness in her heart brought tears welling up. Maggie regarded the girl with quick sympathy, turned and growled at Mike who was taking a nap. Mike woke, growled and whipped his tail.

But I'm not certain they're dead, Greta thought. Maybe, somehow, they survived. I've got to know. I've got to find out. The only answer was to quit the hidden paradise and return to the spaceship.

NOW, HER thinking having grown more facile, other aspects of the picture came to her. She felt, even if vaguely, that her hold over the Hairless Ones could be of great value. Therefore, it was something to be preserved. And, with the appetites of Mike and Maggie to be considered, her goddessship could come conceivably into jeopardy. She felt the Hairless Ones would not too long worship a goddess whose two creatures made a practice of devouring them.

Therefore, Greta told herself grimly, the cats' menus must be augmented elsewhere. Eat they would. That was a definite fact, and Greta was surprised that she did not quaver at the thought of their eating Hagerty's allies, the Tall Ones. After all, this was no tea party. This was a deadly earnest game—survival of the fittest. It was no time to be queasy about the laws of nature relative to Martian tigers.

Having thought it all out carefully, Greta got to her feet and snapped her fingers at the cats. "Come on, babies," she said. "It's time to leave here."

Maggie was eager to go. Mike didn't think so much of the idea, but he complied grudgingly. At the exit door, Greta, having developed a dormant sense of the dramatic, climbed on Maggie, got a good hold, and called: "Open for your goddess. Your goddess would leave this foul bug's nest."

The door opened promptly and Greta gave sharp orders to the cats as she heard Butch do. The response left nothing to be desired. The magnificent Martian tigers went from the room like two orange meteors; out across the green park, knocking the Hairless Ones about like straws in the wind. Up the rocky slope sailed the goddess, triumphantly calm on the back of her tawny mount.

As she reached the high ridge, Greta looked back and smiled. "That," she told the cats, "should give those pigmies something to talk about in the corner tavern."

It was surprising to the girl how a little practice had given her skill in holding her seat on Maggie. Where it had been a perilous chore, it was now an exhilarating experience. She heard herself crying "Faster! Faster!" into the singing wind. She laughed as the great cats dropped seventy-five feet through space to land on a ledge not two feet wide.

Below her now was the comparatively flat floor of the desert and, two miles away, the apparently deserted spaceship. Greta edged Maggie in that direction by pulling hard on the cat's right ear, and in no time at all they came to a halt at the foot of the ramp leading to the open passageway door.

The ramp had not been there previously. Evidently, Hagerty and his Tall Ones had looted the ship; had probably taken the cargo of heavy salt to their factories.

GRETA DISMOUNTED and climbed the ramp. All was silent. She peered into the ship and saw a single light burning in the passageway. Sick with fear at the thought of coming upon the dead bodies of Cort and Butch, she moved forward, down the passageway toward the pilot room. The door was closed. She opened it—and found herself staring up at a Tall One—evidently a guard left at the ship by Korbo or Boss Hagerty.

The man blinked, unable at first to realize his good fortune. An Earth woman. A creature beyond his wildest dreams standing before him. An Earth woman to be stripped and used without interference by anyone. For this privilege, any Tall One would gladly face death afterward.

He reached for Greta, and it was only by a miracle that she escaped him and was able to turn and flee. She got to the door and through it. On the ramp she tripped, and fell headlong, with the sound of the lustful Tall One sharp in her ears.

"Maggie!" she screamed. "Maggie! Mike!"

Then came pure horror. Two orange streaks sailed through the air—two silent juggernauts of death. The last thing the Tall One saw in this life was a pair of open maws and two double rows of glistening teeth. He screamed once. Then he was dead.

Nearby, Greta rolled over and buried her head in her arms. She clamped hands over her ears, seeking to exclude the awful sounds that filled the air. Rank sickness flared through her body, and to dull its edge there came hysterical tears.

The spasm was slow in passing, but finally her slim shoulders ceased to heave, and she could think more or less clearly again. All was silence about her. Raising her head, she peeked over one arm and saw Maggie and Mike lying placidly nearby. Maggie's ears perked up. Mike, not the sentimental type, merely slapped the ground with one paw and went back to his nap. Around the two cats was nothing to indicate any untoward event.

GRETA CLOSED her eyes and partially surrendered to the weakness within her. And, wearily calm now, her mind found one small thing to be thankful for. At least, she told herself, they're clean cats. They have good manners. If they'd been...messy, I don't think I could have stood it.

In a little while, she got to her feet, still weak of body but, strangely enough, stronger in mind. It had been one thing to decide previously that this sort of affair would be inevitable, but quite another to be an eye witness to the doing thereof. But now, having been a witness, Greta had acquired a sort of strength from it. It was still revolting, but evidently, the human mind has depths of power from which to draw. In the battle for survival, even the most horrible occurrences can be tolerated.

"The important thing is to live," she whispered. "That above all. To live and go forward, I must find out what happened to Dad and Cort and Butch, I must. But I've got to be careful. Dash in wildly and I'll defeat my own purpose. I must investigate each step before I take it. If a Tall One ever gets his hands on me, I'm through."

She entered the ship without fear now, and searched about for any possible weapon which might have been left behind. She found none. But she afforded herself the luxury of a change of clothing. She then went down the ramp to where the cats were waiting. She climbed on Maggie's back and dug her heels into the cat's sides. "Up, baby," she commanded. "Back to the hills. We've got to find a secluded place where there's water and privacy. A hideout, I believe they call it."

CHAPTER ELEVEN

BOSS HAGERTY did not trust Korbo. He had never liked the man, and had used him only because he seemed the best of a sorry lot. Korbo, inherently more cruel than most of the larger Pentarians, had served Boss Hagerty well, but mainly because he was watched day and night by the cunning Earthman. Hagerty knew Korbo would have delighted at an opportunity to cut his benefactor's throat.

In spite of his great success on Pentar, Hagerty was lonely for his own kind. He was lord and master of these retarded people, but he had not a friend among them. He had the fear of all and the respect of a great many, but these were poor substitutes for genuine friendship. He could only get that, he felt, from those of his own kind, and he had taken an immediate secret liking to Cort and the redoubtable Butch. They were the sort he had met often at smokers and political rallies on Earth and his heart warmed to them.

He had made plans to include them in his organization almost at first sight, but he wanted to do it right and, according to his philosophies, there was only one correct way to win their friendship and loyalty. In the political jargon that was Hagerty's basic manner of thinking, it amounted to this: Get 'em in a spot and then pull 'em out. Make 'em grateful. Put 'em under obligation and they got to be yours.

That's how he was working with Cort and Butch. They were in the spot now, and all that remained was to pull them out of it. One fine morning, he went about it. During an inspection of Plant Number Two, he kept a sharp eye out for the pair. He spotted them finally, carrying overloaded sacks of material up a sharp incline toward a reducing mill. Hagerty immediately went straight up in the air. He whirled on Korbo, who was showing him about the mill. "What the hell goes on here? Those two men! Get them over here, quick."

Dumbfounded, Korbo signaled to the three guards he'd put over the Earthmen, and they were pushed down the hill to face Hagerty.

The little man's face was crimson. "You trying to put something over on me?" he snarled. "Who told you to put these men into the factory? Talk, and talk fast!"

"Why, you gave the order yourself," Korbo said.

"You're a damn liar! I didn't say that at all. Now, tell me exactly what I did say."

"Ah—ah—you said, take care of these boys—take care of them good."

"And that's exactly what I meant. You're getting too big for your shoes, Korbo. Twisting my words around to suit yourself. These are Earthmen, and nothing is too good for them. Remember that."

HAGERTY turned to Cort and to Butch with an expansive smile. He noted with satisfaction that they'd had a tough time of it. They were psychologically right for the treatment. Handled correctly, they'd eliminate Korbo and step into his shoes with alacrity.

"It was all a mistake, boys. I'm sorry as hell. Here, all the time I thought you were living the easy life. That's what comes when you trust one of these dumb Pentarians.

Come on over to the commissary and get something to eat, and we'll have a talk. A long talk."

With a threatening look at the silent Korbo, he hooked his arms into those of Cort and Butch and hustled them down the street.

"Did you say something about eating?" Butch asked.

Hagerty laughed. "That's what I said. The best in the house. Some way, I've got to convince you boys I had nothing to do with this."

A few minutes later, when seated across from the two men and marveling at the volume of food Butch could cram into his mouth at one time, Hagerty went on: "You boys may be wondering some about me. Maybe you're still a little suspicious on account of I had you worked over there by the Flame Pool. But when you get to know me better, you'll understand. I was fussed up because you lied to me about the girl. I hate lying and disloyalty of any kind, but when somebody goes all the way with me, there's nothing I won't do for him."

Butch nodded understandingly between bites. Cort said nothing.

"I'm looking for a couple of boys like you. Been meaning to get rid of Korbo for a long time, and this piece of stupidity is the last straw."

"There's an old man here named Lansing," Cort said. "The same one you told us had run away. What about that?"

"Lansing—here? Korbo told me he'd skipped out!" Hagerty banged the table with his fist. "See what I'm up against? Lies...deceit! How would you boys like to take care of Korbo right now and step into his shoes?" Hagerty grinned warmly. "After what he's done to you, it would probably be a pleasure, eh?"

"It sure would," Butch agreed.

"I thought so. You boys had enough to eat?"

Cort looked at Butch. "I have. What about you?"

"I guess so."

They got to their feet, and Butch stepped around the table toward Hagerty. Then, he stopped and glanced back at Cort. He said, "I'm sorry pal. I'm damned sorry, but I just can't help myself."

"It's all right. But let's match to see who does it."

"No time," Butch replied.

He hit Boss Hagerty squarely on the point of the chin. As Hagerty back-pedaled, he followed closely and hit him again in the same place. Hagerty went down like a sack of meal. Butch rubbed his knuckles and sighed. "That probably means our finish, but it was worth it."

He smiled dreamily and Cort said, "You're right. It was worth it. Let's get back to work. When the end comes, we want to be found serenely doing our duty, don't we?"

"You said it. Let's go."

KORBO SAT in his office tapping the edge of a sheet of paper against his desk. Written upon the sheet was a death warrant for two Earthmen. A short time previously, Korbo would have been delighted to carry out that order personally. Now, he wasn't so sure.

He was a cold and ruthless man, Korbo, but deep in his slow-moving mind was a spark of admiration for those more courageous than himself. He had hated and feared the blustering little Hagerty for a long time. He'd longed to do exactly what he'd seen done that day. Sitting there, he relived the scene, marveling at it. Two abused, underfed, overworked Earthmen had sealed their doom by knocking the most important man on the planet stone cold. What nerve! What utterly sublime courage. Flaunting a deathless spirit in the face of oppression; laughing into the abyss of oblivion.

Korbo did not want to kill the two men. He wanted to continue admiring them in the living flesh. But there again arose his own fear of Hagerty. Did he dare flaunt this execution order? Did he dare risk his own life by defying Hagerty?

He wasn't sure. It would take a little mulling over. But he was certainly going to take his time in complying with the instruction.

Came the swift Pentarian nightfall and the two Earthlings were still carrying sacks up the hill. "I don't get it," Cort growled. "Is he playing cat and mouse with us?"

"I don't get it either," Butch said. "We should have been cold meat hours ago. Here, it's almost time to catch a couple hours sleep, and we're still alive. What do you suppose gives?"

Cort heaved a sack to his shoulder. "I don't know. We'll just have to wait and see."

BOSS HAGERTY was worried. Strange, disquieting things had been happening on his little planet. A mystery he could not solve had come into being, and he was losing plenty of sleep over it. Scowling darkly, he got up from his chair and paced the confines of his office.

On his third trip around, he was interrupted by the opening of a door, and his horse-faced female Pentarian secretary pushed her ugly head inside. That alone would have been enough to upset Hagerty on even a normal day. But on this day, it was more maddening than usual. "What do you want?" he snarled.

"Lorker, head of your confidential squad, is waiting to see you."

"Well, don't stand there! Send him in."

The woman withdrew her formidable visage and Hagerty grimaced in disgust. "Me having to look at that puss when there's a dish like Greta Lansing loose somewhere on Pentar. When I find that girl—"

Lorker, a poker-faced young Pentarian, walked into the office and stood waiting. He was chief of a group Hagerty had trained for missions he didn't care to entrust to Korbo. And this particular mission was certainly one of those.

"Well," Hagerty demanded, "Any word of her?"

"No, master, but two more of my men have disappeared."

Hagerty scowled ferociously and chewed on his cigar. "Listen to me, punk! I don't like reports like that. They make me mad. I turned this mission over to you because I thought you had the stuff. I left it up to you. All I said was: 'That girl's somewhere on Pentar. Find her.' And you keep coming in and telling me your men disappear into thin air. Just how are you handling this caper, anyhow?"

The tall youth shrugged. "To the best of my ability, master. I send the men out in pairs with orders to scour the country."

"In pairs?"

"Yes. It seems to me that a couple of able-bodied men should be a match for one Earth-girl if they come upon her."

HAGERTY glared suspiciously. "How do I know a couple of your boys haven't found her and stashed her away somewhere for themselves? How do I know you haven't done it?"

"The master has no reason to question our loyalty."

"I suppose you're right, but what the hell is happening to them?"

"I don't know. They go out to cover an area according to instructions and just don't come back. A pair were due in last night. This morning, I personally followed the route they took and found nothing. I went over the ground inch by inch."

"You didn't find any trace of them?"

The Pentarian hesitated. "I found something, but I hesitate to describe it, as it may have no connection with the case."

"Quit being coy. What was it?"

"What appeared to be the tracks of some strange animals. Great footprints the size of five dinner plates laid in a circle. I know of no animal that could make such a track. It disturbs me."

Hagerty pointed a sudden finger. "Say...maybe you've got something. I thought they were full of hop when they told me about those Martian tigers, but it looks like they weren't. It was on the level. So that's what's been happening. Those cats have been eating your boys for breakfast..."

The Pentarian paled at the thought. "But, master. They had guns! And I've gone over the ground. There was no blood."

"Martian cats eat a man like a tabby eats a mouse. There's never any blood. They start at one end and just munch him down. Say...I wonder if that girl is with the cats? She must be. The boys said they saw her riding one of them."

"What are your orders, master?"

"I want that girl, damn it. I'll call out a regiment. Two regiments if I have to. We'll get on the march and comb the planet if necessary."

"Then, you will instruct Korbo?"

"Korbo hell! He'd grab the girl for himself. I'm putting you in charge of this. Use your own judgment, but get results. Use as much of the army as you need."

"Yes, master," and the Pentarian saluted and left.

After he was gone, Hagerty went to the far wall of his office and stood looking into a mirror. "Why," he complained in a hurt voice, "do I have such a hell of a time getting my hands on a woman?"

BUTCH RAISED a weary arm and made a mark on the wall of the cell. "I can't stand much more of this," he growled. "Even if we are still alive a week after we should be dead, I can't stand it. I'm ready to take a swing at the closest guard and go down fighting."

Cort dug his fingers into the itching stubble on his jowls and scratched viciously. "I'm about ready to concede that's the only way to do it. Hit and run. It's a million to two, but maybe at least one of us could run the gauntlet. Even if we didn't, it would be better than this."

"When we go back to work?"

"Right. I'd been hoping for at least half a break, but it doesn't look as though we're going to get it. Wait any longer and we won't have strength to hit anybody."

Butch was going to reply, but at that moment the boulder in the corner of the cell stirred and both men went over to help lift it. When the space underneath was large enough, John Lansing wriggled into the cell like a snake out from under a rock. The boulder dropped back into place and Butch slumped back against the wall, his eyes on the old man.

"What keeps you going, anyhow?" Butch asked. "You've got more courage than any six men I ever met. Why don't you just up and die?"

There was an undercurrent of tension in Lansing's manner. "Hope, my boy. Only hope keeps me alive, and tonight that hope has flared up brightly. There's something in the wind. Something wonderful." He wagged a bony finger at Cort. "Tell me—have you noticed the change lately in the Hairless Ones?"

"I haven't paid much attention to them."

"That's because they've let you alone. They haven't tormented you. Also, they've quit abusing me and have actually grown friendly and told me of things coming over the grapevine. All their hatred is now concentrated on Boss Hagerty, and they don't seem to have any to spare for other Earthlings."

"What about the grapevine?" Butch asked. "What's coming over it?"

Lansing leaned forward, his sunken eyes aglow. "Word of a girl, a fabulous creature whom the Hairless Ones have adopted as a goddess. There is a weird story of how she made their priest disappear into thin air by the power of her magic. All fictitious, of course, but that isn't the point. I think the girl really exists. They say she rides through the sky on two great animals, the like of which the Hairless Ones have never seen. They say—"

Cort and Butch spoke in unison: "Greta and the cats!"

LANSING smiled in pride. "I thought it would dawn on you. Greta, my daughter. She's become the focal point for an uprising of the Hairless Ones."

"Then she isn't dead," Cort exclaimed. "Somehow, she avoided capture and learned to exist on the devil's own planet. She's alive..."

"Do you suppose," Butch asked, "that she's rallying the Hairless Ones into a revolt? What does the grapevine say about that?"

"It is vague on the how and where of the thing, I was unable—"

Lansing stopped speaking abruptly and shrank back in sudden fear. The heads of both Butch and Cort snapped around and their muscles tensed. There was a time of utter silence.

So great had been their concentration on the startling news that they hadn't seen the cell door open slowly; nor had they heard Korbo enter the cell. He moved softly for a man of his size, and now he stood beside the open doorway regarding them in the dim half-light.

"Okay. Oversize," Butch grunted. "Is the firing squad waiting for us?"

"Take it easy on the old man," Cort requested. "He means no harm. He just came in for a chat."

"I would consider it an honor to die with these men," John Lansing said calmly.

For a time, Korbo did not answer. He stood, silently regarding them. "You are a strange race, you Earthlings," he said finally, "Courage seems to be a part of your makeup. That is not so on Pentar. It is not so with me. I am a coward at heart, as are all the rest of my race, and I have a great longing to be a brave man."

"Well, I'll be damned," Butch muttered.

"Lately, I have shown the first glimmer of courage I have ever been able to dredge up out of my being. I have let you live in direct defiance of the master's orders."

"What are you getting at, Korbo?" Cort asked. "You didn't come in here because you like our company."

"On the contrary—I did. I like your company very much."

"Are you sure this about-face isn't motivated by the threatened uprising of the Hairless Ones? You admit you're a coward. Are you sure you aren't just trying to save yourself if things get tough?"

"You're taking a lot for granted," Korbo answered, "but I'll reply to your questions. Frankly, I thought of the same possibility myself. I have always believed a man should know himself thoroughly, and I can safely say the possibility of the Hairless Ones striking back has nothing to do with this decision. You forget that they haven't a chance of success, whatever their actions. Yet, I am willing to fight with them. I will join their cause before the victory is won or lost. Does that convince you?"

"What makes you think they haven't a chance?"

Korbo shrugged. "What makes you think they have? But one more thing—a condition to my turning from my own people. If by some long chance you are able to reach your ship and leave this planet, I would return with you to Earth. I have a great longing to be among people who rate courage as a virtue. Possibly, in a little time, I can learn it from your race."

Butch was bouncing with impatience. "Wait a minute. You mean the Space Wagon? Can it still be navigated?"

"I don't know. I've inspected it, and there doesn't appear to be anything radically wrong. Of course, I don't know too much about such things."

John Lansing was still bewildered about the whole thing. "Am I to understand—" he began.

But the sharp voice of Boss Hagerty over-rode that of the old man as Hagerty and two armed Tall Ones crowded into the cell.

"All right, boys," Hagerty snapped. "Cover them! We'll make short work of this little clam-bake!"

CHAPTER TWELVE

GRETA LANSING had developed into a strangely dual young woman during the time she had run wild across Pentar in the company of her two great cats. Dual in that she was both happy and unhappy at the same time.

Relative to her father and her companions of the space trip, she was bitterly unhappy. She had devised no way of helping them—in fact, had not even been able to discover where they were being held or if they were still alive. This frustration and uncertainty was with her day and night, and she upbraided herself for lack of ability to take advantage of the good fortune which was hers. It seemed to her that a goddess should be able to promote a little security for those she loved. But even armed with divinity so far as the Hairless Ones were concerned, and armed more realistically with Maggie and Mike, she could still devise no way to make use of them.

On the other side of the picture was her new-found sense of freedom, which amounted to intoxication. It was a heady thing to ride like the wind across Pentar on the back of the swift Martian cat. It gave her a sense of delicious power to exert a control over these two magnificent beasts. In the deep rocky fastnesses of Pentar, she had worked diligently to make the cats even more subservient, and she had succeeded well. Even the truculent Mike would leap down a hundred-foot gorge to spring back with a stick in his mouth. Maggie would roll over and play dead upon order, and both cats would stop dead in their tracks at a command from Greta.

The problem of food had not come up, forage having been thoughtfully provided by Boss Hagerty. It seemed that each day at mealtime a pair of grim, gun-toting Tall Ones turned up on schedule, so Greta had never found out if a hungry Martian tiger would eat a friend when famished. Both Maggie and Mike became most proficient in bringing down an armed man. There would be a period of quiet stalking while Greta hid in a convenient cave; then a quick whirlwind rush and it would be all over.

Greta had avoided the Hairless Ones also, mainly because she didn't know what to do about them. They were hardly people she cared to pal around with, and somehow she felt she should keep her escutcheon of goddess clean and shining by the glamour of absence. She had seen several of them peering out at her from various vantage points as she traveled over Pentar, but she had always passed them by like a beautiful nymph on an orange and black cloud.

THERE CAME a day, however, when this situation changed. Upon this day, she was lying in a grassy nook by a spring pulling dreamily at Maggie's whiskers, when two Hairless Ones popped their heads from behind a rock nearby. Both Maggie and Mike sniffed lazily. They had known full well of their presence before the little men had appeared, but the cats exhibited only lazy contempt. They were entirely satisfied with their diet of Tall Ones.

Greta half expected the Hairless Ones to flee in terror, but they did no such thing. Their fear was outwardly apparent but they came forward nonetheless, crawling along on their bellies with their noses brushing the ground.

The girl waited in interest for their next move. Mike raised his head and growled a warning, but Greta silenced him with a command and asked:

"What do you want?"

The ugly little monsters trembled, but one of them got up courage to speak. "Our people beaten down—in bondage. Unhappy."

"That's too bad. Is there something I can do?"

There was a new trembling in both men now, and Greta recognized it as eagerness. "Hairless Ones would fight," the spokesman said. "Fight good for their freedom. They need their goddess to lead. Goddess could free them. Free others in factories, too."

"Others? What others?"

"Earthlings held to work in factories."

Greta sprang forward and grasped the man by his thick arm. "How many Earthlings? What do they look like?"

The man cringed and put his face against the ground, but he spoke up clearly: "Three—all men. Two young— big. One most old—hardly alive."

A feeling of quick gratitude swept through Greta. She wanted to cry and laugh and shout to the hills for joy. They were still alive! Dad and Cort and Butch! Still alive, even though held in the grip of Hagerty and his awful Tall Ones!

"Of course we will free them!" she cried. "We will free all Pentar!"

At that moment, there was a sudden diversion as a squadron of some fifty Tall Ones came swiftly into view from beyond the rocks. From where they stood, the tableau of the beautiful girl, the cats, and the two Hairless Ones was visible as though on a stage.

THE TWO Hairless Ones cringed and whimpered. Greta herself would probably have been terror-stricken a few moments before, but now things were different. She was full of fire at the tremendous news.

Drawing herself up like a goddess, she spoke to the Hairless Ones: "Be not afraid. Merely sit on those rocks and watch. Then, return and tell your friends what you saw."

The Tall Ones, recovering from their surprise at stumbling upon their quarry, let out a joyous whoop and started up the slight incline toward Greta. The girl spoke sharply; "Maggie! Mike! Take 'em! Take 'em, babies! Clean 'em out!"

The terrible Martian cats rose up in all their ferocity. With twin screams of rage, they swept from a lazy crouch into projectile-like movement, and were upon the Tall Ones before the men could raise a weapon.

Nothing in all creation is so devastating as a Martian hill cat when the killing lust is upon it. At least ten of the Tall Ones died during their first moment of frozen terror. The rest dispersed in panic. Two of these fell, and the cats began to mop up.

Now, Greta really tested for the first time her absolute power over the cats. "Stop! At rest, Maggie! Hold it, Mike! Come back! Come lie down!" She called out the commands with no great expectation of their being obeyed. But Maggie dropped instantly to the ground, rubbing her belly in the dirt and snarling. Then, she turned and came trotting back up the incline. Mike also dropped what he was doing and looked at his mate as though he thought she'd gone daft. Then he, too, came back to the family circle.

The Tall Ones were gone in panic. They would carry the word, Greta thought. Possibly other Tall Ones, upon hearing it, wouldn't be quite as good soldiers as they had been.

And the Hairless Ones would also carry the word. This she instructed them to do, "Go to all your people and tell them what you have seen. Tell them to assemble at the temple by the colored pool. I will come and lead them! Go!"

A few seconds later, the Hairless Ones had vanished also. Left alone, Greta did not feel quite so much like a goddess. Turning from the gory sight below, she dropped to her knees and buried her face in Maggie's shoulder. The cat turned her head in inquiry as Greta wept.

CHAPTER THIRTEEN

AS HAGERTY stepped into the cell, both Cort and Butch had the same thought at the same instant. This was it. Sure death, if something wasn't done quickly. Without a word, they sprang forward, and so closely were they in rapport, that they functioned as a team without losing a second.

Butch dived for the closest guard, while Cort went straight for Hagerty. He had to get the little Boss quick or they were through, because there was another guard to contend with. He drove a straight left at Hagerty's chin that, had it connected, would have sent the man into dreamland. But Hagerty moved enough to dull the blow.

Cort cursed his luck. No chance now. The other guard had had the second of time he needed to raise his gun. Viciously, Cort swung again at Hagerty. He was at least going to get one in before he went down. This time, the blow connected perfectly and Cort spun around to face the gun he knew was leveled.

But he was wrong. He had erroneously reckoned without Korbo. The second guard lay sprawled on the ground with Korbo rubbing his knuckles. "What do we do now?" the Pentarian asked blankly.

"Get the hell out of here!" Butch barked. "You're still in command out there. You can order them to let us through."

"I can't do that," Korbo replied as Butch's mouth dropped open. "I will fight my way out with you—die with you if necessary, but giving false orders would be treachery. I am a soldier, not a traitor."

Butch turned to Cort in amazement. "What goes with this guy? Is he nuts? I don't understand."

"He said he'd fight with us. Isn't that enough? Let's get started."

They filed swiftly out of the cell as Korbo said, "There shouldn't be too much trouble. Very few guards will be about. If we just go quietly."

But there was no quiet to be had. Other plans had been afoot—sinister plans—because from everywhere there appeared shadowy forms of Hairless Ones to join the group until it swelled into the dozens. Three guards appeared, to be cut down by the guns in possession of Cort and Butch.

Then, there were several others who, when they saw their allies slain, fled in terror.

"I told you all the Tall Ones are cowards," Korbo said.

"Then what's all the fuss about?" Butch wanted to know. "Cowards don't fight."

"They are craven, but they will win the last battle. Evidently, the Hairless Ones are assembling in response to some call for action. But they are helpless because they have no arms. When the final battle is fought, the Tall Ones will move like a solid wall spouting green death. The Hairless Ones will be beaten down."

"Okay," Butch replied. "But it's a swell way to die."

"That's what I want to learn," Korbo said with deadly seriousness, "the ability to view things with that kind of courage."

"You're nuts," Butch said, but his tone was friendly, and there was a grin on his face.

THE HAIRLESS Ones seemed to know where they were going. They tended to ignore the Earthlings, but suffered them to come along as the squat little men babbled in their own tongue and seemed to glow with a great hope.

Dawn shot up over the horizon, and Cort could see several hundred of the small men, a fair-sized army.

But this army, it developed, did not arrive in time to join the battle. They got there only in time to function as spectators. As they came over a long rise, the plain before the rock pile housing the Flame pool, was spread out before them. On the rocks and along the base of them, were several thousand Hairless Ones.

Moving in across the flats was what Korbo had predicted—a solid wall of Tall Ones moving against the revolutionists. Each man carried two deadly guns—an impenetrable wall of death.

"See," Korbo said sadly, "It is as I told you. What chance have the Hairless Ones?"

"They'll have a better chance if we can get there to help them," Cort said. "Let's go."

The group started to run and Korbo with them, but shaking his head in bewilderment the while. "I can't understand it," he said. "Men walking into certain death and eager to get there."

At that moment, the Tall army opened fire. Streams of deadly green flame poured into the Hairless Ones, cutting them down by the dozens.

"The damned murderers," Butch screamed. "Can't we do something?" In desperation, he poured his own fire at the killers and succeeded in stilling a couple of the guns.

Then, a strange thing occurred. Down the rocks from above came two great Martian tigers, screaming and roaring out their hatred. On the back of one rode a girl who looked like a goddess. Head thrown back, the wind streaming through her short hair, she called out for courage among the Hairless Ones.

The cats sailed over the massed unfortunates in a single great leap, and streaked straight toward the wall of death.

And the wall faltered. The green fire fizzled away as the terrified Tall Ones forgot their deadly weapons in the face of their fear—fear of this terrible goddess they'd heard about.

Greta dropped from Maggie's back and strode to encourage the misshapen little fighters to again take up the war. This while the cats began a fearful slaughter of their own. Thus, the tide of battle turned. I was all over in a short period of intense bloodshed. The Tall Ones had swiftly lost a war.

"THANK GOD the ship's okay," Cort said. "We'll take this stinking little ward heeler back to Earth with us. He's got to face a murder rap."

In handcuffs, Hagerty rolled his cigar and was noticeably glum. "It was a sweet racket," he said. "I'm damned if I can see why you had to stick your nose in and break it up."

"Shut up, half-pint," Butch said. Then, to Korbo, "But you, my friend, are not going back with us. You're staying here."

The Tall One put out a hand in protest. "But you promised."

"Yes," Cort said, "but things have changed. Word is out that you're needed here. The Hairless Ones trust you and the Tall Ones, I think, have learned a lesson. This planet needs a wise head to chart it over the rough spots to come.   Also, a courageous man," Cort added with inflection.

Korbo's eyes opened wide. "You mean—"

"I mean this: There is nothing you can learn about courage on Earth. In fact, you could probably teach us a few things."

"It's all very bewildering," the Tall One said seriously. "Very bewildering."

A short time later, Cort walked with Greta near the big ship that would take them back to Earth. It was the first time he'd really gotten her alone since the great battle. He felt a trifle awed, a little uncomfortable. "There—there are quite a few things I'd like to say—"

She came close. "Why don't you just kiss me, darling?"

Cort was kissing her again sometime later when Butch hove in sight. Butch grinned. "Love's grand, I guess, but it's not for me. Guess I'm unlucky that way."

He grinned, and called back over his shoulder, "I still got my cats."

Greta smiled sweetly and called back: "Are you sure about that?"

THE END

If you've enjoyed this book, you will not want to miss these terrific titles…

ARMCHAIR SCI-FI & HORROR DOUBLE NOVELS, $12.95 each

D-111   **THE MOON ERA** by Jack Williamson
REVENGE OF THE ROBOTS by Howard Browne

D-112   **SON OF THE BLACK CHALICE** by Milton Lesser
SENTRY OF THE SKY by Evelyn E. Smith

D-113   **OUTPOST ON THE MOON** by Joslyn Maxwell
POTENTIAL ZERO by S. J. Byrne

D-114   **OUTPOST INFINITY** by Raymond F. Jones
THE WHITE INVADERS by Ray Cummings

D-115   **TIME TRAP** by Rog Phillips
THE COSMIC DESTROYER by Alexander Blade

D-116   **THE OTHER SIDE OF THE MOON** by Edmond Hamilton
SECRET INVASION by Walter Kubilius

D-117   **DANGER MOON** by Frederik Pohl
THE HIDDEN UNIVERSE by Ralph Milne Farley

D-118   **THE WAILING ASTEROID** by Murray Leinster
THE WORLD THAT COULDN'T BE by Clifford D. Simak

D-119   **THE WHISPERING GORILLA** by Don Wilcox
RETURN OF THE WHISPERING GORILLA by David V. Reed

D-120   **SPECIAL EFFECT** by J. F. Bone
WARLORD OF KOR by Terry Carr

ARMCHAIR SCIENCE FICTION CLASSICS, $12.95 each

C-37   **THE GREEN MAN RETURNS**
by Harold M. Sherman

C-38   **THE SHAVER MYSTERY, Book Five**
by Richard S, Shaver

C-39   **MARS CHILD**
by Cyril Judd

ARMCHAIR MASTERS OF SCIENCE FICTION SERIES, $16.95 each

MS-7   **MASTERS OF SCIENCE FICTION AND FANTASY, Vol. Nine**
Poul Anderson, "The Star Beast" and other early tales

MS-8   **MASTERS OF SCIENCE FICTION, Vol. Ten**
Robert Moore Williams, "???" and other tales

If you've enjoyed this book, you will not want to miss these terrific titles...

If you've enjoyed this book, you will not want to miss these terrific titles…

ARMCHAIR SCI-FI & HORROR DOUBLE NOVELS, $12.95 each

D-131 **COSMIC KILL** by Robert Silverberg
BEYOND THE END OF SPACE by John W. Campbell

D-132 **THE DARK OTHER** by Stanley Weinbaum)
WITCH OF THE DEMON SEAS by Poul Anderson

D-133 **PLANET OF THE SMALL MEN** by Murray Leinster
MASTERS OF SPACE by E. E. "Doc" Smith & E. Everett Evans

D-134 **BEFORE THE ASTEROIDS** by Harl Vincent
SIXTH GLACIER, THE by Marius

D-135 **AFTER WORLD'S END** by Jack Williamson
THE FLOATING ROBOT by David Wright O'Brien

D-136 **NINE WORLDS WEST** by Paul W. Fairman
FRONTIERS BEYOND THE SUN by Rog Phillips

D-137 **THE COSMIC KINGS** by Edmond Hamilton
LONE STAR PLANET by H. Beam Piper & John J. McGuire

D-138 **BEYOND THE DARKNESS** by S. J. Byrne
THE FIRELESS AGE by David H. Keller, M. D.

D-139 **FLAME JEWEL OF THE ANCIENTS** by Edwin L. Graber
THE PIRATE PLANET by Charles W. Diffin

D-140 **ADDRESS: CENTAURI** by F. L. Wallace
IF THESE BE GODS by Algis Budrys

ARMCHAIR SCIENCE FICTION & HORROR CLASSICS, $12.95 each

C-58 **THE WITCHING NIGHT**
by Leslie Waller

C-59 **SEARCH THE SKY**
by Frederick Pohl and C. M. Kornbluth

C-60 **INTRIGUE ON THE UPPER LEVEL**
by Thomas Temple Hoyne

ARMCHAIR SCI-FI & HORROR GEMS SERIES, $12.95 each

G-15 **SCIENCE FICTION GEMS, Vol. Eight**
Keith Laumer and others

G-16 **HORROR GEMS, Vol. Eight**
Algernon Blackwood and others

HE PLAYED FOR POWER IN A FORBIDDEN CITY OF FREE MEN

Dr. Simon Kirk was a true company man. He was the divisional director of the mighty Cominc Corporation, and many felt that at age thirty-one he was much too young to hold such a lofty position. But his future seemed bright, and he was smugly satisfied with himself. In fact, his overall brilliance had put him in line to become the next president of the company.

Then one day a strange interruption in communications service led him to a distant relay station that lay many hours away in the sprawling wastelands that had once been the United States of America. Inside this remote building Simon Kirk met his destiny; and slowly he changed from an obedient executive who held power over legions of mindless slaves, to a leader in a hidden city of free men. But whether that city could survive or not remained to be seen, as the long arm of the world's corporate cartel reached out to smother and destroy it.

CAST OF CHARACTERS

DR. SIMON KIRK
He was as brilliant, and as high up the company ladder as anyone thirty-one years of age could possibly be.

ARTHUR C. BELCOURT
The news reports of this legendary scientist's death had been extremely exaggerated.

ELLEN BELCOURT
On the surface she appeared to be just another pretty face behind an information booth, but there was much more to her than that.

WINGATE
Recently promoted from Captain to Commandant, he'd been in the service for years and liked to bellow a lot.

GENERAL KIRK
His own son had thought him dead for many years, but he was alive and well and helping to build a city of free men.

MacNAIR
Loyal to the core, he was as loud and blustering a Scotchman as had ever been known in a world of non-thinking citizens.

BRYANT
He was a hard-working quartermaster on a large airship, but he had secrets—secrets he guarded very carefully.

FRONTIERS BEYOND THE SUN

By
ROG PHILLIPS

ARMCHAIR FICTION
PO Box 4369, Medford, Oregon 97504

*For more information about Armchair Books and products, visit our
website at…*

www.armchairfiction.com

Or email us at…

armchairfiction@yahoo.com

CHAPTER ONE

GRAMPS STRETCHED hugely, then settled back in his chair again. Lighting an old-fashioned cigarette, he inhaled deeply and glanced at the sun-filled countryside. Fresh spring air blew softly across the porch where he sat, bearing with it the smell of growing things.

Billy, his grandson, looked up from his studies. "What started the Age of Centralization, Gramps?" he asked.

Gramps pursed his lips. "Kind of hard to say. Order to know what started it, you'd almost have to get into the minds of the men responsible. How far are you in modern history?"

"I'm just past the Second World War."

"Do you understand how that war started?"

Billy nodded. "I think so, Gramps. At least, it seems pretty clear. The part that I simply don't understand is why everyone got together the way they did."

"Well, that's hard to explain too, Billy, without going over a lot of dog tails and that would take a lot of time."

Billy shrugged his shoulders. "I haven't got anything to do, Gramps. I'd kind of like to hear about it. You never have talked much about the past."

"I guess I haven't," Gramps admitted, "but I don't usually think too much about it. The history of the world is a pretty sordid affair up until the Reclamation."

"Come on, Gramps," Billy coaxed. "I've got to write a thesis on this next month and I sure can't do it with the material I've got now."

"Well, I—don't really know where to begin," Gramps said hesitantly.

"Why don't you start with the property system? That's something I don't understand either. How did the tycoons get other people to give them those big fabricating plants?"

Gramps chuckled. "Well, they didn't exactly give all that land and equipment away. It worked something like this. In those days, a man was born into this world with nothing, he was educated in publicly owned schools and, when he got to be a young man, he would go out and look for a job."

"You mean he'd sell himself into voluntary slavery?"

"That's about it," Gramps replied, "but he had to. The employer, as the tycoon was called, actually didn't have any authority. A man would agree to work for him for so many hours and he would receive so many certificates that were good in trade."

"Those certificates were called money, weren't they, Gramps?"

"THAT'S RIGHT, son, and there certainly was all kinds of it. Well, let's get back to our young man. Let's suppose he worked for eight hours a day and yet he made enough money or trade certificates in four hours to exchange for all of his needs. Then, half of what he earned, he could save by giving his certificates to a bank to keep for him."

Billy nodded. "I follow you so far, Gramps. Go ahead."

"Well, each year, the bank would pay this young man interest, as it was called. That is, they would give him two or three percent of his sum in the bank in addition to what he had saved. This was given in return for the privilege of letting the bank use his money for that year."

Billy sighed. "I don't see how the banks could get very far doing that."

Gramps laughed. "You can take it from me, they did. The banks would loan this money to people, who needed it and charge them a small sum for its use. The sum that they charged borrowers was quite a bit more than what they paid out as interest."

"You mean the banks didn't do anything but just sit and pass other people's money back and forth? They actually didn't do a thing productive?"

"That's right," Gramps smiled, "but we're digressing. Let's catch up with our hero. Years have gone by now and our young man has grown past middle age. He's been saving everything he could and he's been earning more and more money as his experience makes him more valuable to the tycoon. Then one day, our man goes to the bank and takes out all his money and looks around for a place to invest it. That is, he wants to put it somewhere where it will pay him more than it does in the bank. Let's suppose he goes up to see his own employer. He says to him, 'See here. I've worked for you for many years and I've saved all this money. Now I want to be a business man like yourself.'"

"Well, his employer looks at the money and says, 'My business is worth twenty times what you have here but I'll tell you what I'll do. I'll sell you one twentieth of this concern and I'll put you in charge of part of the business." Our man likes this idea so he does it and, from then on, he's no longer an employee. He's a tycoon."

BILLY'S FACE mirrored his lively interest.

"After the Second World War was over," Gramps continued, "the secret of atomic energy was known but it was kept by the military and it was several years before they let the world use it. Even then it was under such crippling restrictions that no one knew much about its management. The country I was born in was on the verge of a revolution or civil war. The first users of atomic power were given wide publicity in the hope it might prevent the coming revolt. I remember only vaguely the headlines in the newspapers as, one after another, the big industrialists were given permission to use atomic power. For a while, we all thought it was the beginning of a new era and, in a manner of speaking, it was."

"The national work week was cut down and there was plenty for everyone. But, only the big tycoons were given permission to use atomic power and, little by little, they forced out the little businesses. The little ones couldn't afford to compete with the big ones so they went into bankruptcy or, in most cases, sold their holdings to the big companies. Along about this time; we began to notice that the forests were dying and things just wouldn't grow. Some scientist declared that he had found a new particle in the atomic structure and this particle was the one that was killing all the trees and plant life."

"That was the nucleatron, wasn't it?" Billy asked.

Gramps nodded. "That was it, all right, and it was there, too. The big corporations said there wasn't any such thing and went right on using their unshielded power generators while the rest of the folks sat around and watched the forests disappear, the meadows become barren and the whole of the North America turn into a desert. While this was going on these big companies were merging with other big companies until they were too gigantic to even imagine. With the soil dead and unproductive, the companies were even the only producers of food. Then, little by little, they extended themselves until they had a grip on the whole world.

"There weren't any real governments. To be sure, they still had names but the companies had the power. Finally, there were only five big corporations, Power, Inc., Transportation, Inc., Communications, Inc., Food, Inc., and Fabrication, Inc. There wasn't one small business in the entire world, not even a pencil peddler. Every man, woman and child, even new-born babies, was technically, an employee of one of these colossi. A man was born and raised and died in the service of one company whose service he could not leave without inviting starvation. There was no recourse to law except the company's law and the company's police force. There were no elections; there was no individual freedom. Yet, there was no want and almost everyone was satisfied because he didn't know any better.

"The companies traded freely among themselves apparently in perfect harmony with no one infringing on another's field. But underneath, there was tension, strain and distrust and, occasionally, people would disappear, never to be heard from again. The population was concentrated in huge cities with most of the land a desert. The companies didn't do anything to correct this because it gave them an iron grip on the people of the world. The biggest of these cities was Transinc I, which was on the narrow neck of land that joined what once had been North and South America. From the air it gleamed like a box of jewels. It was over a hundred miles long and fifty miles wide and stretched from sea to sea. Great resilient roads, thirty lanes wide, led to the north and south carrying the goods of the world by land. Harbors stretched the length of the city on both sides of the isthmus. In each of these great harbors, giant cranes lifted the complete cargo section out of the immense ocean carriers and trundled them overland swiftly on their beryl-nickel rails. Some of these sections were stacked like cord wood in gigantic, roofless warehouses but others were carried the complete fifty-mile trip from ocean to ocean and, there, fitted neatly into the hulls of other cargo carriers.

"IN SPITE of the massiveness of the works involved, the noise was hardly audible and even the giant cranes rolled over their diamond-hard rails with only a sigh of wind around their straddled legs.

"To the south of the city, twelve overhead mono-rail cargo trains sped swiftly to and from the great air terminal. This great man-made plateau, six hundred square miles in area, saw the daily arrival and departure of over ninety thousand air and strato craft. These varied in size from single-place atomic jet planes to the mammoth gravity-beam-supported strato liners.

"The metropolitan center of the city was a circle approximately twenty-five miles in diameter in which almost half of the three hundred million employees of Transinc were housed. The remainder of the employees were located in the eleven subsidiary transportation centers throughout the world. Almost in the very center of the city, in the shadow of the eight-hundred-story Transinc administration building, stood the one-hundred-story Cominc building, the outlet for Communications, Inc. It was directly connected to the equally vast city of Cominc, surrounding what was once San Francisco bay like a huge mouth preparing to engulf a tiny morsel. The connection was an intangible, invisible beam stretching like a thread through the Cominc relay station to the disbursement center in Cominc. As compared to the huge blue and white buildings of Transinc, the Cominc building was small. It stood out only by the bright swirling red and yellow of its plasto-marble shell."

CHAPTER TWO

ON THE top floor of the Cominc building, Dr. Simon B. Kirk, the Divisional Director, sat in his palatial offices. He was young to be the holder of such an exalted position, only thirty-one. His brilliance and achievement in pioneering the polar automatic relay stations had put him in line to become the next president of the company. His future was assured and he was smugly satisfied with himself. His vigorous outdoor life had left its mark. He was tall, bronzed, and had steady blue eyes. His dark hair held just a suggestion of a wave which he hourly tried to remove with a comb.

He leaned back in his chair looking at the panoramic view of the immense city through the wide panes of transparent plastic that formed the walls of his offices. This also enabled him to see the balance of his offices yet remain unseen himself. He musingly watched the golden sunset and the lights, winking on all over the city like earthbound stars. His rosy dreams of the future were interrupted by the melodious signal of his desk 'visor. Simon touched the gleaming chromium bar at its base and the 'visor sprang into brilliant life. The normally untroubled face of the District Chief Engineer appeared before him with tight lines of worry around his eyes.

"Yes, Heisman. What is it?" Kirk asked brusquely.

"I don't like to trouble you with the problems of the engineering department, sir," Heisman began, "but we've had service interrupted four times this week. We can't find anything wrong with the relay station and I was just wondering, sir, if you would mind giving me a hand. I don't mind admitting I'm stumped."

Simon Kirk's momentary annoyance didn't register on his face. "After all," he reflected, "this is part of my job." Aloud, he said crisply, "Not at all, Heisman. I'll be down in three minutes."

With a flick of his finger, Simon turned off the 'visor and got to his feet. Punctually, three minutes later, the gravity lift lowered him to the first sub-level of the Engineering Department. He stepped through the maze of controls that operated the vast communications center and into the Chief Engineer's office in time to catch the last words of the Chief Engineer who was speaking to one of his assistants.

"—if the big shot doesn't get in the saddle. I'll bet he doesn't know that service was off for thirty seconds yesterday."

Kirk answered tranquilly, "Indeed I do, Heisman. In fact, I sent a memo to the Chief asking for an inspector to check on the trouble."

Heisman's jaw set grimly. The arrival of an inspector would mean that he would be removed from authority until the investigation was over. "There wasn't any need of doing that, sir," he said plaintively. "I'm sure I can find the trouble if I'm given a little more time."

"You've already had a week," Kirk answered stiffly, "and you are only allowed four days under company law to find interruptions. You should have notified me three days ago if you wanted to avoid an investigation."

HEISMAN said nothing and handed the small bundle of blue interruptions-of-service sheets to his superior. Kirk studied them intensely and then looked up.

"The inspector won't arrive until tomorrow but I'll go out to the relay station tonight. The monitors show no breaks here or in Disbursement. If I can find the trouble and correct it tonight, I won't have you relieved. Otherwise..."

Kirk left the thought unfinished and abruptly left the room. He turned as he reached the gravity lift. "Remain here in the office," he ordered. "I'll contact you at 0130." Then the lift whisked him out of sight.

There was a slight haze around the air terminal and dew was beginning to settle as Kirk walked across the grassy sward to the control tower. He stepped through the doorway onto the escalator and rode to the top of the tower. The control chief was listening intently to weather reports and didn't notice Simon's entrance. He stood by the door waiting for the chief to finish his listening. In a few minutes he snapped off the instrument and turned to see Kirk standing there.

"Why, Dr. Kirk! I didn't hear you come in." The man smiled brightly and extended an enthusiastic hand. "Certainly glad to see you again. Remember the time I was commanding that strato liner? Boy, I sure thought I was going to wrap that boiler around a mountain! I would have, too, if you hadn't found my position. I don't know how you Cominc boys do it!" he went on still pumping Kirk's hand with Homeric gusto. Simon was taken aback by this verbal monsoon.

"Ah—, of course, of course, —ah, happy to see you again Captain—, ah—" Kirk racked his brain but all he could think of was Windbag.

"Wingate! Don't tell me you've forgotten your old pal Captain Wingate. Only it isn't Captain anymore. It's Commandant Wingate now! Lots more credits every payday. Say, how about doing the city with me tonight? I'm off in an hour. Nothing's too good for my old pal!"

At this point, Wingate punctuated his sentences with violent blows on Kirk's unprotected back. Such pulmonary and muscular development is only attained by ship captains after decades of service.

Kirk's purpose leaped to mind with the aspect of a life preserver to a drowning man. "I'd love to, some other time though, Commandant," he began tactfully, "I've got some work to do tonight. I'm going out to the relay station and I'd like to use a Transinc messenger 'copter instead of one of our own. I'd like to do a little scouting around without being noticed."

"NO SOONER said than done!" the older man bellowed. The Commandant drew a red flight order out of his desk and, after quickly perusing the flowing auto-file, dropped the sheet into the machine and pressed one of the multitudinous buttons on its surface. The auto-file purred briefly and made clucking noises like an over-maternal hen as it automatically recorded flight data on the sheet. The hum died and a white release card slid out of a slot bearing all the pertinent data about the craft. At the same instant, the service man in the hangar would be receiving instructions on a 'visor about preparing the ship for flight.

"I wonder," Simon said hesitantly, "if I could keep this a secret? You know the company rules don't allow me to operate another company's equipment without special permission."

"Surest thing in the world," exclaimed Wingate, and he added his own name to the card with a laborious flourish.

Kirk reached for the proffered card just as the Commandant launched into an anecdote about his colorful past that threatened to assume the proportions of Buckle's "History of Civilization." Simon tried a hasty retreat toward the escalator but the older man followed him in hot pursuit, the walls echoing and re-echoing to the heroism and sagacity of the redoubtable Wingate. Finally, the escalator carried Kirk away from the ever-mounting din at the top of the tower.

Simon walked rapidly toward the hangars, glancing over his shoulder apprehensively as if in fear of being overtaken by the braying Commandant in his resplendent uniform. The silence was almost oppressive. At last he reached the hangars and, inside, the service chief glanced briefly at the four silver embroidered triangles on the lapels of Kirk's jacket. He received Simon's card with a deferential nod and crisply led him outside to a blue and white messenger 'copter whose overhead blades were still folded.

"There she is, sir," the service chief announced. "Will there be anything else?"

"NO, THANK you," Kirk replied. He settled himself in the cockpit and fastened the plasti-glass bubble tightly over him. He noted with some relief that the craft was practically identical in design to his own company's. A brief touch of the master switch and the great blades unfolded overhead. The atomic motor's ham raised in pitch. Simon pressed the takeoff button and waited for an answering note through his loud speaker from the control tower. Then, a great wave of sound swept over the plane, penetrating its nearly soundproof body.

"Hi there, Dr. Kirk!" The bemedaled figure of the Commandant charged across the field toward him like a gold-braided rhinoceros.

Viciously, Kirk ramped the ascension lever to its full position. With a surge of power, the craft leaped upward. Soon the buildings below took on the proportions of toys but, even then, Simon imagined he could still hear the stentorian tones of the ex-captain.

Kirk adjusted the controls and set the auto-pilot for the four-hour trip. Darkness completely cloaked the earth and, as the lights of the city were swept away behind, only the instruments gave indication that the craft was moving at all.

Simon amused himself with the ship's televisor, listening and observing the three-hundred piece symphony of Power, Inc. This program was succeeded by an insipid episode from the daily life of an equally insipid characterization of motherhood. The observer was left in no doubt that this was presented by the Crystol Soap Division of Food, Inc. The announcer stressed three times the spelling of the word, Crystol. With a vague feeling of nausea, Simon snapped the 'visor off and decided that the program was the greatest inspiration for UN sanitation he had ever heard. The heroine of the story could only have achieved her present mental state by eating as well as washing with the stuff. Kirk comforted himself with the thought that listeners of public entertainment had suffered under the same drivel from soap manufacturers for longer than he could remember.

He wondered whether or not the 'visor would pick up an Eastern Hemisphere station and switched it back on. The set responded promptly by bringing him the face and voice of an E. H. announcer. He was prattling in rapid-fire Russian and reminded Simon of a machine gun with inflection. His limited understanding of Russian couldn't hope to cope with this so Kirk retuned the set to the local station.

The local entertainment channel had just ended the daily episode of the soap program. It was one of the few sponsored programs on the air. Kirk had tuned in just in time to hear the announcer say, "C-R-Y-S-T-O-L! Crystol! The soap of Crystol purity!"

Soon a group of amateurs appeared and presented Shakespeare's "Julius Caesar," It was wholly uninspired but inoffensive. Just as one of the characters completed a hammy "Et, tu, Brute," the screen broke into a display of pyrotechnics. Geometric shapes and shadows flitted across the screen; polychromatic, amorphous shapes were born and died too quickly for the eye to see their outline. There was blackness for an instant, and then the stage sprang into view again. Someone stood over Caesar, looking for all the world as though he would give vent to a Tarzan yell of triumph. Caesar was now stretched out full length, making horrible gasping sounds.

Kirk turned the set off and stared at its blank, idiotic face. "Interruption number five!" he muttered. "And what an interruption!"

IT WAS UNLIKE anything that Simon had ever seen. His concentration was broken by the sharp warning of the landing signal and the craft began to descend rapidly. He cut the automatic controls and landed the ship directly in front of the relay station.

At first, everything seemed perfectly normal. Then Simon noticed, with a queer feeling in the pit of his stomach, that the door of the station was slightly ajar. He reached inside of his jacket, detached the tiny needle gun and removed the safety. Opening the hatch as quietly as possible, Kirk jumped down to the ground. To Kirk, the crunching of his boots on the sand was loud enough to wake the dead. Gently, he toed the door open, holding a small inspection light in his left hand and the needle gun in his right. No matter who or what it was, he was confident that one or two anesthetic charged needless would render it *hors de combat*. The sharp beam of the inspection light swept over the interior of the building and came to rest on the face of a middle-aged man.

The man's voice was deep and resonant. "You needn't shoot," he said calmly. "I have my hands in the air."

Kirk watched him intently as he snapped the emergency lights on. The man was tall and looked strong in spite of his advanced years. His snow-white hair was thick and was swept back in a smooth pompadour. His dress was much the same as Kirk's except for the heavy holster that hung at his hip. Simon gingerly disarmed him before speaking.

"You know that this is an offense punishable by death, don't you?" Simon asked heavily, indicating the man's atomic blaster, which he had just lifted. "Every company has a law against possession of one of these. You also know that being within one hundred feet of this building is punishable by death."

"I had only to pull the trigger on that and I wouldn't have to face execution," the man pointed out. "You were clearly outlined in the doorway."

Kirk regarded him in speechless puzzlement.

The man continued. "If you had been in a company plane, I would have fled before you landed. As it was, you did catch me off guard but I reasoned correctly that only a high official of Cominc could obtain the use of a Transinc craft. I thought it would be worth gambling my life to talk to you. I haven't too much to lose. I'm getting old."

"Just what did you want to know that's worth risking your life for?" Simon asked cautiously.

"I didn't want to ask you anything," was the reply. "I wanted to tell you something, Dr. Simon Bolivar Kirk…"

Kirk raised an eyebrow. "You know me?"

The man chuckled softly. "Doesn't everyone? You were quite the pioneer a few years back."

Simon smiled in spite of himself. "How did you know I'd come here?"

"I didn't. I hadn't even hoped you would. I just knew it would be somebody up in the top brackets."

"WELL," KIRK prompted somewhat impatiently, "what was so important?"

"If you please," the intruder asked, "may I lower my arms? They're growing awfully tired. I assure you I'm unarmed."

Simon studied him briefly and then nodded his assent.

The stranger replied, "Thank you. Now as to my purpose, first I must tell you that I'm not an employee of any corporation. I didn't like being a slave like you."

Kirk colored slightly and barked, "I'm not a slave. I'm a Divisional Director..."

The white-haired man waved his hand as though dismissing the interruption. "No one can tell me what to do," he went on, "and neither can anyone kill me if he feels like it in my own land."

"Your own land?" Simon repeated blankly.

"Do you think everyone is content to be a slave?" the man asked gently.

Kirk bit out, "I repeat...I am not a slave..."

"Oh, yes, you are," the man contradicted, "a high-salaried, straw-boss slave but a slave none the less! The company can break you just as easily and quickly as it could its lowest worker."

Simon's face became a brighter crimson. "That's the third offense punishable by death," he snarled, "trying to undermine our company governmental system!"

"Can they shoot me three times?" the man asked with grim humor.

"Go on," Simon said gratingly, "you must have something else to say. You can't just be trying to make your death a certainty for nothing!"

The intruder smiled a little. "I admit I'm not more anxious to die than you are but I'm afraid that I don't seem to be converting you too easily. Possibly I banked too much on your name."

Kirk's puzzlement must have been apparent for the stranger elaborated.

"Have you never heard of your namesake, Simon Bolivar? I've always been one of his greatest admirers. In fact, reading his life led me to become a free man."

It would be untrue to say that Kirk had never heard of Simon Bolivar but the name aroused only the vaguest response in his consciousness.

"As a matter of fact," the stranger added, "I've carried that book with me as a good luck charm ever since I read it. It looks like the charm has run out, though, so if you'll accept it, I'll give it to you."

The man reached into the pocket of his jacket and Simon's hand tightened on his gun. The man brought forth a small, leather-bound book and Simon's hand relaxed. He accepted the book without comment, glanced at the cover and noted the plainly printed title, THE LIBERATOR.

Simon began to wonder what he was going to do with this man. He had been accused of being both cruel and tyrannical but he liked to think of himself as just and humane. Simon tried rationalization. "After all," he reasoned, "this man is calm and convincing but his sentiments clearly show him to be insane." That was it! INSANE! Just a harmless lunatic in spite of the blaster.

KIRK RECALLED the tales he had heard of men on isolated patrol duty losing their minds. The explanation was brilliantly simple. He felt a sudden sympathy for the demented man.

"If you promise me one thing," Simon began cautiously, "I'll not take you back with me."

"Go on," said the man with an inscrutable smile.

"If you'll promise never to go near a Cominc relay station again and give me the key you used to open this door, I'll let you go free," he finished.

"Sounds fair enough," the man assented, handing him a small gleaming key.

"All right, you can go," Kirk said. When the stranger reached the door, Simon stopped him and handed him the blaster. After all, he couldn't leave him unarmed in this barren wilderness that had once been the United States. Besides, he had to dispose of the blaster in some way. Its presence would be hard to explain.

The man bowed his head a little, accepted the weapon and departed.

SIMON BEGAN an inspection of the station to see what damage there was, if any. After nearly forty-five minutes of searching, he found nothing, nothing, that is, except two tiny marks like scratches on the windings of the modulator coil. It wasn't until then that Kirk remembered the strange images he had seen on the screen. Had a coil merely been shorted, it would have produced no image, only blankness.

"Probably some kind of hazy experiment the man thought up in his moments of loneliness," Kirk mused to himself. He gave a quick glance at his chronometer. "0126," he said aloud. Quickly turning off the lights, Simon locked the door. He walked out to the waiting ship, absently dropping the key into his pocket on the way. Seating himself once more in the craft. Kirk pressed the call button on the 'visor. The Cominc operator's pleasantly impassive face appeared. Her eyes widened as she recognized her superior.

"Your connection, sir?" she inquired. Simon heard the stranger's voice in his brain repeating. "SLAVES!" He squelched the thought abruptly.

"Get me Cominc, 109." He paused, then added, "please."

The operator's face looked downward for a moment, then the view snapped to the face of the Assistant Engineer.

"Heisman, please," Kirk requested.

The assistant averted his eyes for a fraction of a second and said in his ingratiating voice, "Mr. Heisman was taken ill, sir, and had to go home. May I serve you in any way?"

"No—I guess—not." Simon answered slowly. "That's all. Good night."

The assistant smiled briefly before his face disappeared.

Kirk frowned in speculation. He'd be willing to bet that Heisman wasn't sick. He aroused himself and prepared the ship for flight. As he took off, he hoped he could catch a few hours' sleep before arriving home. He would need some in order to face the inspector tomorrow.

CHAPTER THREE

PROMPTLY at 523, the landing signal sounded again rousing Simon from his fitful nap. He stretched and looked below. The machine had performed its duties faithfully for it was suspended a thousand feet above the field. He signaled the control tower and the controlman's sleepy face lighted the screen, perfunctorily giving directions for landing. The background of sound around the controlman carried no highlights of Commandant Wingate's blaring voice, which gave Simon a profound sense of relief. Certainly he was in no mood for any blustering joviality.

The craft lowered itself gently under Kirk's guiding hand to its preordained spot. He had hardly unfastened the hatch when a three-man crew took charge and whisked the plane from the landing area to make way for others. Already the tremendous activity of the day was beginning.

Kirk walked from the paved hardness of the field onto the grassy lawn at its periphery. Debating momentarily, he decided the walk to the metropolitan transitube would clear his mind. After fifteen minutes of walking, a soothing scent assailed Simon's nostrils. It appeared to be a mélange of ham, bacon, eggs, pancakes, toast and coffee. Although he knew the odor had been synthetically compounded in a laboratory and shipped to the restaurant in a bottle, it was none the less appealing.

"Probably the old man who broke into the station would disapprove of Syntharoma also," Kirk said half aloud. Oddly enough, he had forgotten about the meeting of the night before until now. Still, the average company official who has to endure an inspection is liable to think of little else. With the thought, Simon thrust his hand into his jacket and withdrew the book he had been given. He turned it over in his hand meditatively as he entered the automat. The brightly lighted interior was deserted. Simon scanned the vise-menu briefly and pressed buttons to indicate his selections. While he waited for the mechanism to serve him, he opened the cover of the little brown book. Inside, on the title page, he found: THE LIBERATOR, The Life of Simon Bolivar. Below this, inscribed in a fine hand, was, "This book gave me a new life at fifty. Arthur C. Belcourt." Kirk read no further. He was stunned.

"Belcourt!" Simon knew that he had been lost at sea eight years ago. And this was incredible. How could the old demented guard have gotten this book? Unless, of course, it might be a forgery.

SIMON REACHED into his pocket again and found the key he had carelessly dropped there the night before. Now, on closer examination, he could see that it wasn't an ordinary stainless-steel key. On the shaft of the bit of metal he could discern tiny engraved letters, "A. C. B., from Cominc".

Kirk remembered the strange story of how the key came to be made. A meteor had fallen some twenty odd years ago and it was composed of some metal that defied analysis. It was harder than diamonds and couldn't be melted at any temperature available. Yet, in a powerful magnetic field, it softened enough to be worked and immediately hardened when withdrawn. The tiny specimen, which had been tested in the laboratory, had been made into a master key and presented to Arthur C. Belcourt, who was then the Research Chief of Cominc.

Simon studied the bit of metal for a moment. "Could this be the fabulous key?" He withdrew his ring from his finger and held it with its small diamond between his thumb and forefinger. He selected a small point of the stone and brought it sharply across the haft of the key. It left no mark. Then this must be it! But then, how did that old guard—but wait... He had only assumed that the old man was a guard. No...that couldn't have been Belcourt! If it was, why should he conceal himself? A scientist as great as he could step right back into his old position at any time and there would be no questions asked.

At that moment, Kirk's meal arrived and slid smoothly onto the table from an overhead carrier. He ate measuredly, reading the book from cover to cover in hope of finding a clue to the mystery. Speed reading had been developed to a science in the last few years. Simon scanned the pages, absorbing the Material at more than a thousand words a minute. When he was finished, it could not be said that he understood the book thoroughly but his semantically trained reflex patterns stored the material accurately. Within a few hours, his understanding of the book and its contents would be as complete as though he had studied for days under the old system.

This absorption and coordination process was well under way when he left the automat. It was only a short walk to the metropolitan tube. At the tube station Simon entered a waiting carrier and settled himself for the forty-five minute journey. Shortly, the carrier began its headlong flight to the city center. Throughout the trip, his meditation went on. At the terminal, he proceeded on foot to the Cominc Building, still in deep abstraction.

Inside the building. Simon made the journey to his office before divorcing himself from his intense concentration. The logic was simple and inescapable. It must have been Belcourt that he saw last night! Yet that did not explain his presence at the station.

SIMON GLANCED at his chronometer. 744. He would have just enough time to freshen up a bit before the inspector's arrival. He pressed the "no admittance" button on his desk, automatically locking all doors. Stripping off his synthoid garments, he tossed them into the disposal chute, carelessly. It hummed briefly and, a moment later, from the slot beside the chute, a fresh outfit appeared, containing all his belongings in the proper pockets. Simon stepped into the "fresher cabinet." Warm cleansing solution deluged his body and was followed by fresh water. Warm air ducts dried him as the massage stroked his body to brisk aliveness.

As he stepped forth from the cabinet, and donned his fresh uniform, the work looked considerably brighter. Already plans began to formulate in his mind for the solution of this mystery. The planning was short-lived for the door signal sounded. Simon glanced again at his chronometer. 800. Punctual was the word for Cominc officials. He pressed the "open" button on his desk. The automatic locks slid back and the door opened.

Immediately, a gasp of pleasant surprise escaped Kirk's lips. "Roger! Well, Roger Lourde!"

"Hello, Sim," the fat man in the doorway replied. "Surprised to see me?"

"Surprised? Don't tell me you're the inspector that I've been worrying myself gray-headed over?"

"Yup, I'm a big shot now," Lourde chuckled. "I got too big to clear transmitting towers and too slow to run around the office so they had to make me an inspector."

"Well, congratulations, man," Simon responded. "I always knew you'd make the grade anyhow."

"Thanks, Sim," Roger grinned. "You always were my biggest booster."

"Say, if the company had seen you work the way I did on the Arctic station, they'd have boosted you up five years ago."

Lourde's jovial face sobered a trifle as he replied, "Thanks again, Sim, but much as I hate to put a stop to all these compliments, I've some very serious stuff to take up with you this morning."

"You mean the interruptions? Well, I've got those all taken care of. It was just a little leak in a condenser that the usual test missed. It would build up an overload and then let it go, blanking out the circuit. I just happened to see it or I'd have missed it too."

Roger's face was grave and the silence was noticeable before he answered. "Sim, you and I have known each other too long to beat around the bush. I know all there is to know about those interruptions. I suppose I shouldn't tell you this but I've been here since 330. Just before I came up here, the Chief Engineer came to see me."

Kirk raised his eyebrows. "I thought he was sick in bed."

"No," Lourde replied. "After talking to him, I'm the one that's sick. I appreciate loyalty to the company but what that guy gave me this morning is strictly loyalty to himself. It sounded and looked good but he didn't know I knew you. I'll be honest with you Sim. Unless you tell me the truth about everything you did last night, I'll have to put you in detention and recommend trial for treason."

SIMON WAS speechless. "Treason! I don't know what you mean!"

Lourde shifted his bulk on his chair. "This man, Heisman, followed you out of here last night and took a portable videograph with him. I saw the record this morning. I saw you go into the control tower, come out, and go down to the hangar. I saw a close-up of the card and your name wasn't on it. You got into a Transinc 'copter and flew up to the station. You went in and, a couple of minutes later, Heisman stuck the video lens into a ventilator slot and I saw and heard you talking with a man. I couldn't see him because the slot was in the way but I heard him and, take it from me. Sim, any judge that saw and heard that record, would send you to the disintegration chamber. The man's face was turned away when he came out and Heisman didn't follow him for fear of being seen but, no mistake about it, that was you on the record."

Simon was aghast with horror. He realized how damaging that record would look to any outsider.

Lourde went on. "Nothing you could say would change that record or keep you from being executed but there's one thing I want to know. Are you trying to pull something funny or are you on the level? I mean, are you connected up with any sort of underground movement?"

Simon found his voice. "Of course not, Roger…"

Lourde weighed this in his mind for what seemed an eternity. "Sim, I'm not going to say whether or not I'd do what you did last night, because I'm not supposed to be a judge. I'm a human being and I can understand a lot of things but some of our judges aren't so human and I think if I were in your place, I wouldn't want to chance not finding a human judge. No, I think, if I were you, big and strong like you are, and all that was standing between me and freedom was a fat man that doesn't get enough exercise—" He let the thought trail off.

Kirk looked at Roger intently. "You mean—" Roger nodded his head.

Simon took a deep breath and said huskily, "Thanks, Roger."

Lourde silently handed him a pair of glittering handcuffs. Simon quickly manacled the fat man in his chair.

"Better gag me too," Roger suggested dryly.

Kirk did so as quickly as possible. From the doorway. Simon turned. "I don't know where I'm going but I'll bring back that man that broke into the station and I'll find out where his group hangs out—if it takes the rest of my life!"

Lourde nodded his head impatiently toward the door.

"Thanks again, Roger. I'll square myself somehow," Simon said just before he opened the door.

His trip to ground level was made in an agony of suspense. At any moment he expected the lift to stop but it didn't. No one seemed to take any particular interest in him outside of their usual courtesy. The new girl at the information desk smiled dazzlingly at him but he was too distracted to notice. The girl continued to smile even after he had left the building. She pressed a combination of buttons on her 'visor. A man's face flashed into being.

"He's on his way," she said briefly.

"Good," he replied. "I'll be at the station."

"What shall I do?" the girl asked. "Shall I just disappear?"

The man considered this and then nodded his head. "Yes, I promised your father that I'd take good care of you. You can go back the same way you came. It's still perfectly safe. If you stay there through the investigation they might suspect you."

"All right, George," she answered.

In a few minutes, with her hat at a jaunty angle; she vanished into the immense city.

CHAPTER FOUR

IN SPITE of the fact that the metropolitan tube speed was well in excess of one hundred miles an hour, to Kirk it seemed to be carrying him away from the city center at a snail's pace. The trip outside the building had been difficult enough but at least outside he could move around, dodge or hide. Here, in the carrier, he was imprisoned. For all he knew, it might be carrying him into the hands of the company's law. His only hope of escape lay at the air terminal and that was based on Commandant Wingate's obvious friendship. Indeed, the sight of the blustering old man would be welcome. There were too many unknown factors to deal with, so a planned escape was out of the question. How Simon envied the split-second accurate judgment of fictional heroes.

Since there was no immediate threat to his life. Simon found much time for speculation. The high, plaintive whine of the carrier's AC electro magnets blotted out all extraneous sounds, leaving Kirk in a world of his own. He had waited in the metropolitan tube terminal until no one sought to occupy the five-man carrier he now rode. For the present, at least, he was withdrawn from the eyes of the rest of the world. For the present.

Even though Wingate might have been warned by now, there was a strong chance that he would still cooperate. That is, if Wingate was on duty! The thought was an alarming one. Suppose it was a stranger or worse still, a man who knew him by sight! Strange, he had not thought of this before but it was too late now to turn back. He had to go through with it.

Simon loosed the needle gun from its small holster. It was fully charged. Well, anyway, that remained as a last resort. Of course the possibility was strong that some of the men he would have to overpower would be armed.

A sudden hiss of compressed air signified the end of the journey. The carrier slowed rapidly and drew to a smooth halt at the end of the tube. Simon stepped out into the small underground station, gratified that it was empty. The automatic escalator immediately started and carried him to ground level.

Outside the terminal were three auto taxis. He climbed into the front seat of the first and fished in his pocket for a half credit coin. This he dropped into the meter on the instrument board. A small green light on the meter indicated that the taxi was ready to go.

Ten minutes later, Kirk parked at the air terminal. Although an automatic record of his face had been filed in the meter of the taxi, he was untroubled. They would trace him to the air terminal soon enough anyway. He refused to consider the idea that they might already be waiting for him.

He ascended, unaccosted, to the top of the control tower. His hand gripped very tightly the small needle gun in his pocket. At the top of the tower, he stepped into the Commandant's office. Simon felt an immediate sense of relief when he saw that Wingate was there. The Commandant's grizzled head was sprawled on his arm on top of his desk. He appeared to be sleeping. A very much diminished bottle of Scotch rested beside him. On the floor, a completely diminished whisky bottle leaned at a crazy angle against the desk.

KIRK SHOOK the Commandant gently without result, then more firmly, still without result. The Commandant was too large a man for more vigorous measures. A slight smile curled the corner of Kirk's mouth as he leaned down to the Commandant's ear and shouted. "Captain! She's out of control!"

Wingate reached up from the desk like a bear would if he sat on a hot stove. "Emergency stations!" he bellowed. "Man the lifeboats! Empty the forward fuel tanks! Heave—" The bellowing stopped abruptly and Wingate regarded Kirk with a bleary s tare. "Hey, lad!" he roared affectionately. "Don't do that to a man!"

In spite of himself. Simon laughed. " 'Tis not so funny as you think, my boy," Wingate resumed. "I was having a dream and I was on the bridge again. I was just givin' landin' orders to my mate when you yelled in my ear. You like to cut ten years off my life!" Wingate relapsed weakly into his chair.

Simon's hearty laugh died away into a broad smile. "I'm sorry, Commandant," he apologized, "but it seemed the only way to wake you up."

"Ay, lad, it woke me up right enough. But unless I miss my guess, you won't be waking up Commandant Wingate anymore. By this time tomorrow, my boy, I'll be Deckhand Wingate! Take my word for it!"

Simon regarded him incredulously. "Deckhand Wingate?"

"Yes, Deckhand! They're going to bust me," he replied lugubriously. "The Director's office called this morning."

"It isn't about that ship you loaned me is it?" Simon inquired.

"No, my boy. That was perfectly legitimate. Yesterday, I signed the routing papers and dispatched a transport to Power City. Then, last night, I got special orders to bring it back. It had contraband of some sort on board. My men and I couldn't find it and couldn't raise it on the video. We ain't seen hide nor hair of 'em since. The Field Commandant at Power City swears up and down that he never saw the ship or the orders. The Director thinks I've been shipping contraband but they can't prove it. Otherwise, they'd shoot me. As it is, they gave me twenty-four hours to get that ship back, or else!"

"And you haven't been able to find it at all?" Simon asked. "Not even wreckage?"

"Not a sign!"

Kirk whistled softly through his teeth. "That is bad," he muttered. "What sort of contraband was she carrying?"

"I'll be blasted if I know!" Wingate replied. "All I know is that it was plenty hot." He regarded Kirk in silence for a moment and then resumed. "Simon, my boy, you've known me for quite a long time, off and on. You know I wouldn't do a thing like that, don't you lad? They didn't put me here because I was the smartest Captain they had, but because I was honest. Would you—maybe—testify for me at the inquiry? With someone like you to put in a good word, they might not bust me."

SIMON SIGHED. "I can't, Wingate," he said softly. "I've been charged with treason by my own company."

"My gawd!" exploded Wingate. "But they can't do that! Not to you!"

"They have," Simon answered.

With a shrug of his shoulders, Wingate accepted his fate. "Well, lad, shall we go out and do the town while we've got the time?" he asked with a half-hearted smile.

"I'm afraid I haven't got even that much time," Kirk said. "I escaped from an inspector and left him tied up in my office."

"Lad! You've got to get out of here!" Wingate announced abruptly. "Here! I'll get you a fast plane." He reached toward the flight order forms.

"No!" Kirk stopped him. "In your predicament, they'd send you to the chamber if you helped me."

Wingate's hand hesitated. "Are you innocent, my boy?" he asked.

"Yes," Simon replied.

"Suppose you had a little time," the Commandant inquired, "do you think you could prove it?"

"I think so."

"Good enough!" Wingate exclaimed. He rose from his desk and fed a flight order into the auto-file.

"I can't let you do this!" Simon protested.

"Don't worry, lad. I'm going with ya. Don't you think I deserve a chance to prove my innocence too?"

Kirk looked at him in astonishment. Wingate was transformed into a whirlwind of activity. He made five calls on the 'visor in rapid succession. To each, the same cryptic remark was made. "Special mission T-338. Immediately. Have your gear and be ready to go in half an hour!" To each call, a different voice replied, "Ay, Captain" or "Yes, sir."

The calls completed, Wingate left his desk and lumbered to the laundry slot beside the 'fresher cabinet. He jabbed the service button viciously until he had exhausted the supply of uniforms. Then he sprang to the closet and emptied it of its contents which he draped over his arm along with the uniforms. Lastly, came the Captain's bag into which the clothes were hurled unceremoniously. The bag was snapped shut and heaved over his immense shoulder. He stopped in front of Kirk. "Hmmm. You look about the size of my Chief Assistant," he remarked. Kirk was dragged precipitately behind the hulking figure to the escalator.

"What—!"

"You'll see!" Wingate roared.

They entered an unoccupied office. Wingate went through the same emptying procedure that he had just finished in his own quarters. At last he jammed a bulging bag into Simon's hands. "Here, lad. You're a sailor now."

THEY PAUSED at the door. Wingate withdrew his wallet and counted out a thousand credits, which he laid on the unoccupied desk. "That ought to buy him a new wardrobe," he chuckled, and they left the office.

Once again they rode downward on the escalator. At the bottom of the tower, they went through a door marked "Ready Room." Inside, Wingate bellowed, "Pull off them duds, son. We gotta look like sailors!"

Simon obeyed, wonderingly. The Commandant explained as they changed clothes, donning uniforms they had brought in the bags. "Them groundhops on the field can't see no further than the stripes on your sleeve but we gotta look the part if we want to get away with this."

The Commandant studied himself briefly in the mirror, nodded his satisfaction and then began fishing in his bag. He came up with a sealed box which he tossed to Kirk. Reaching in again, he produced another for himself.

"Just hold on a minute, lad, and I'll rig you out after I get myself fixed up."

Wingate emptied the gleaming contents of the box into one of his hands. With a dexterity born of long experience, he affixed the insignia to the lapels and breast of his uniform. With the same dexterity, he pinned the insignia on Kirk's uniform. He stood back and appraised Simon for a moment and then shoved him before a full length mirror.

Simon felt ridiculous in the resplendent uniform but he reflected that it was probably necessary. Wingate instructed him briefly in the procedure.

"My men will be by the ship when we get there. Walk in front of me until you reach the gangplank. Then come to attention and return the salute of the men who will be waiting. Do a right face and salute me. Stand at attention until I'm aboard the ship, then you follow me. That's all you have to do, but for God's sake do it right! You're supposed to be my Second in Command. Think you've got it now?"

Wingate gave him a demonstration of the proper salute and stance.

A slight smile touched Simon's lips. He saluted briskly. "Yes, sir!" he replied.

"Good boy!" Wingate roared, banging Kirk on the back. "Now let's get going…"

Outside the building, they could see a huge strato ship with the gleaming T-338 on its bow.

"That's it," Wingate muttered out of the corner of his mouth. "Now go to it."

Simon took his cue and marched toward the ship. It couldn't have been more than three hundred feet, but to Simon it seemed to take hours before they stood in the shadow of the hull. As he returned the salute of the five men lined before the gangplank, he waited in an agony of suspense for a hand to be placed on his shoulder or a gun to be thrust into his back. Wingate seemed untroubled. He returned Simon's salute and walked through the port, serene of face. Simon followed him as rapidly as he dared. His feet had hardly touched the decking inside when he heard the dural gangplank being drawn inwards.

THROUGHOUT the ensuing activity, Kirk stood motionless by the portal until Wingate's bellow snapped him out of his indecision.

The gleaming walls rang with the sound. "First Officer Kirk. Front and Center!"

Before Kirk had a chance to think, he was running headlong for the front of the ship. In the gadget filled control room men were efficiently disposing of their duties as they made adjustments, pressed switches and observed instruments. Wingate's eyes didn't stray from the master control panel. Finally, he seemed satisfied and jammed a large red button on the side of the board. Instantly bells began to ring throughout the ship and varicolored lights went on all over the control room. The decking quivered slightly under Simon's feet, then it lurched. They were under way.

Kirk watched through the curved transparent panels that formed the nose of the ship. Fragile though they looked, he knew that nothing but a head-on collision could ever damage them. The field dropped away under them quickly. The great nose swung around and faced what he judged to be west. The throbbing of the deck plates increased in intensity and the force of acceleration sought to throw him backwards. He grasped the handrail for support.

Many minutes passed before Wingate was satisfied with the performance of the ship and pulled the red locking bar on the controls. The men at their stations did likewise with theirs.

Wingate turned from the panel. "Markham," he ordered crisply. "Take the first watch."

"Yes, sir," echoed the tall, thin man who had been standing at the ascension controls. The rest of the men left.

Now that the strain of the takeoff was passed, Wingate resumed his joviality. "Simon, my boy," he rumbled. "It's time you got acquainted. This is Chief Navigator Markham at the controls."

Markham turned his head long enough to nod. "How do you do, sir."

"I'm not sir," Kirk protested. "I'm only along for the ride."

"As long as you wear that uniform with the Captain's permission, you're the Second in Command," Markham contradicted without looking away from the controls.

"He's right," Wingate grinned. "You're a real sailor now."

Simon was horribly embarrassed. "Any of these men," he protested, "could do the job better than I could."

"Uh-uh," Wingate replied. "The law says that the Commanding Officer of a ship must be a graduate engineer and that just leaves you and me. And don't tell me you don't have an engineer's degree."

"But I don't know how to command a ship," Simon protested.

"Now, my boy, I happen to know very well that you went through Transinc's Air School before you took charge of Communication there."

"Well, yes," Kirk admitted. "I can fly a 'copter, that's for sure."

"Lad," Wingate explained. "Our Chief Engineer can't navigate, the navigator can't fix the engines, the Quartermaster can give us air, food and water but he can't navigate. Same goes for all the rest. Besides, there's an old law that says if a man is transferred to another company, he must be given a station of equal or greater authority than the one he left. The one you got ain't as good as the one you left…"

KIRK SHRUGGED his shoulders. "The only thing you haven't got," Wingate added, "is the proper procedure for Officers in Flight. And every officer's cabin has a copy of them rules, so if you want to be a *real* sailor, just go down and bone up on 'em."

Simon couldn't be sure but he thought he detected a trace of a smile on Markham's face. He turned back to the Captain. "Well, since I am destined to be Second in Command, can I know our destination?"

"Damn if I know," Wingate answered. "If you got any suggestions my boy, make 'em!"

Simon became thoughtful. "Well sir—"

"Don't keep calling me *Sir,*" Wingate interrupted. "Markham is too much in the habit to break him. Besides, there isn't much point in being formal now."

"I think," Simon began again, "or that is, I have a hunch that your disappearing ship and my disappearing company official are tied together in some way."

"What disappearing company official!" Wingate bellowed.

Kirk briefly outlined his encounter of the previous night. He ended with, "So you see, Captain, I'm convinced that was Arthur C. Belcourt I talked to and somebody wanted me out of the way so I couldn't reveal that fact. Naturally I would mention it in my own defense at the trial. Oh, sure, I know the man who let me escape but I don't know who suggested it to him. It all seemed so logical then but I wasn't given time to think it out until after I had escaped."

"Yeah," the Captain admitted. "It does look kinda like one of those put-up jobs but that doesn't answer my question. Where are we going?"

"The only thing I can suggest," Simon answered, "is to make it appear as though we crashed at sea and then go to the relay station and see if we can trace Belcourt from there. He must have come in a flier and if we can find his landing tracks, we'll know from what direction he came. We might find a clue inside the station if we search carefully. There isn't anyone living within a thousand miles of the station so I'm sure we'll be safe."

"I still don't quite see how our troubles are connected, my lad," Wingate stated dubiously.

"I admit the logic is pretty thin," Simon answered, "but you remember I said Belcourt professed to be part of a hidden group and it would take a fair-sized group to waylay a transport. If the transport had gone down at sea, you would have found traces."

"Yeah, I know," Wingate said, "and I'm certain she didn't go down at sea."

"A transport is too big to hide anywhere except in a city," Kirk continued, "and if it were in a city, everyone would have to be in on the plot to hide it, even the representatives of the other companies."

"About the only place that's left," Wingate commented, "is some remote spot somewhere, maybe even an island, but it would take us years to search for it. Besides, if we ever got near the regular shipping lanes, we'd be spotted for sure."

Simon thought for a few minutes. "I'm afraid the only hope I can offer is to search the station. If we can find out where Belcourt came from and where this group of his is, we might be able to find the ship. At least, that's a good place to start."

"YOU MIGHT be right, lad." Wingate turned to Markham. "What do you think, Markham? You're in this too."

"Whatever you say, sir, is all right by me," Markham answered without turning his head. "I'm glad enough to be on the bridge again without asking questions."

"Very well, then," Wingate said. "Release a crash marker."

Simon, watching through the transparent panels, saw a small, red cigar-shaped object plummet away from the ship. It spun lazily downward and struck the surface of the ocean with a splash. A brilliant yellow spot began to spread on the top of the water. This patch of color would persist for days and, if found by searching ships, it would be evidence that some craft had been lost at sea.

"What are the coordinates of that station?" Wingate asked abruptly. Kirk rapidly gave him the geographical position of the relay station.

"Did you get it?" the Captain inquired of Markham.

"Yes, sir!"

"Set our course and speed accordingly! We don't want to land before 2300," Wingate instructed.

"Yes, sir!"

The ship began its slow swing northward. Wingate touched the communicator stud. "MacNair, Bryant, Anderson, Barronoff. Assemble in the mess hall." He snapped off the switch and turned to Simon. "Come on, my boy. Let's combine business with pleasure. We'll get a little chow and you can meet the crew at the same time."

Simon followed Captain Wingate down the companionway.

CHAPTER FIVE

THE MEAL prepared by the ship's automat was indeed satisfying, particularly in view of the small size of the unit. Simon leaned back in his chair, the inner man comfortably filled. As had been the custom of sailing men for generations, nothing but small talk had passed around the table during the meal. Kirk now found it true that the future looked much better on a full stomach.

Now that all were finished and the machine had removed the last vestiges, Captain Wingate leaned back in his chair and lit a cigar. "Oops, forgetting my manners, boys," he said, passing around the plastic container filled with smokes. The men each accepted one and so did Kirk. He sniffed the aromatic stogie and raised his eyebrows in approbation.

"Two credits apiece," Wingate remarked with a pleased smile. "Not likely to be any more for a while so might as well use 'em up."

As Kirk inhaled the fragrant smoke, Wingate cleared his throat noisily. "I think it's about time I started letting my hair down, boys. Your First Officer here is the famous Dr. Simon B. Kirk of Cominc."

A slight stir went around the table. Then the gruff voice of the Chief Engineer, MacNair, interrupted. "Canna be. Wingate me man, thut because yourrr own education wuz neglected thut we canna recognize the face of a famous man when we see it?"

"If you ever saw his face before, it was over a borrowed 'visor, you tight fisted Scotchman!" Wingate roared.

"Dinna be castin asperrrsions on the name of MacNairrrr, ye overrrstuffed windbag!"

"It seems to me, you glorified grease monkey, that you've forgotten the last time I threw you down the gangway into your dirty engine room!"

"Thut does it!" clamored the Chief Engineer. "Forrr yearrrs I ha put up with yourrr dirty insults, but now ye imply thut the engine room of MacNair is like a hog pen! Coom ootside! Weel settle this man to man!"

Simon was stunned but no one seemed to take any regard of this uproar but him. The others finished their coffee and cigars as though the two belligerents didn't exist.

Kirk could stand it no longer and leaped to his feet. "Gentlemen, please... We have important things to discuss."

"Ha ye no fearrrs," MacNair replied calmly. "I would na hurrrt the big lout. He's a bonnie Captain in spite of his ither defects."

This goaded Wingate further. "Why you wizened up miserable skinflint," he growled. "Just wait till we're alone... I'll beat some respect into ya if I have to pound your brains out against one of your precious engines."

MacNair was fully as large as Wingate and Simon couldn't have called him wizened up even in the wildest stretch of his imagination. His lined face and tousled hair gave him an appearance of ferocity that was not at all in keeping with his character.

THE THIN, scholarly looking man at Simon's right who had been identified as Bryant, the Quartermaster, gazed at the two men over his cup of coffee, weighing his words carefully. "To the best of my knowledge, this bickering has been going on for more than fifteen years and I fail to see that either of you has subdued the other. Do you suppose if I were to provide you with guns that we might get it settled once and for all?"

Anderson, the First Engineer, who sat across the table, ran his thick fingers through his blond mane and in a voice like the deepest tone of an organ thundered, *"Shuddup!"*

The power of the voice made the table shake under Kirk's fingers. At least, here was a voice with greater power and resonance than Wingate's.

Barronoff, the Signal Officer, stroked his neat black beard and remarked cordially to Simon, "For men of our intellectual attainment, Dr Kirk, it is distinctly disturbing to be in such an atmosphere. Don't you agree?"

Simon didn't have a chance to reply.

"I would na be referrin' to intellectual attainment, if I, werrre in yourrr place, ye a man thut signs his name wi an X."

Barronoff polished his immaculately manicured nails on his equally immaculate sleeve. "You may have some trouble, Dr. Kirk, in understanding the speech of my erstwhile comrade from the lowlands of Scotland but I shall be glad to act as interpreter at any time."

"All right, lads," Wingate bellowed. "Let's stow it for now. We don't want to be giving Dr. Kirk a bad impression of us."

"Ya!" echoed Anderson.

Bryant's soft voice interposed. "Don't mind this too much, Dr. Kirk. We have found formal discipline too trying on a long voyage and the first day is sort of an ice breaker. The only one who doesn't join our camaraderie is Markham. He's always rather shocked at our conduct. I doubt if you'll believe me but we're really quite a smooth running little organization."

Simon relaxed and smiled. "I agree it was something of a shock. I'd always pictured you ship officers as being a sternly disciplined bunch."

Bryant laughed. "I'm afraid that's all show. The days of iron discipline went out with Captain Bligh. Nowadays, we're more technicians than sailors, particularly on ships like this."

"Yes," Simon replied. "I've noticed that the ship seems to have no crew other than ourselves."

"This baby's almost entirely automatic," Barronoff said. "She doesn't need anything but men to control the various functions. Of course, if there's a breakdown, there's a little more dirty work than there would be if I had a few assistants."

It was plain that Barronoff didn't care for what he called 'dirty work.' Simon smiled at the thought of Barronoff grubbing around in the innards of the ship with his immaculate fingers and getting grease on his immaculate uniform.

Wingate laid an affectionate hand on Simon's shoulder. "I guess it's about time we let 'em in on the secret, eh, boy?" He turned to the others with a broad grin. "Men, Dr. Kirk and I are a couple of hunted criminals…"

MACNAIR shook his head. "Tsk-tsk-tsk. I always knew ye would come to a no good end. Weel, it's too late now. Ye might ha the courrrtesy to tell me in whut ye has involved me."

Wingate glared at the Chief Engineer.

"I'm afraid it's all my fault," Kirk interrupted. He briefly recounted his experiences to the men, ending with, "Then Commandant Wingate decided to go with me to see if we couldn't find some clue to establish his innocence too."

MacNair looked at Simon thoughtfully. "I can weel underrrstand yourrr predicament, lad. It could happen even to MacNairrr. I dinna blame ye one bit, but this ignorrramus at the head of the table has to loose a transport! 'Tis inexcusable!"

Wingate squirmed but could think of nothing to say.

Bryant gnawed at his knuckle and gave Kirk a penetrating look. "Are you convinced that the man you talked to at the station was the missing Belcourt?"

"That's the only explanation," Kirk replied simply.

"Even if it wasn't him," Barronoff added, "he certainly must know something of his disappearance to be in possession of that key. May I see it please?"

Kirk handed it to him. Barronoff tried the same test that Simon had. The bearded man studied the key. "It's certainly the one," he remarked incredulously.

"I'm sorry you are involved in this," Kirk said. "It's a very serious matter and, if we are caught, you'll probably be imprisoned."

Bryant laughed. "Our part in this is quite simple, Dr. Kirk. Captain Wingate called us and told us to sail and since we have all been on the beach for a long time, we jumped at the chance and didn't ask questions. We'd get off pretty well with that story."

"Just a minute," Barronoff interrupted. "We no longer have our commissions, you know, and sailing a ship without one is termed piracy. What's more we knew it before we sailed."

Wingate regarded his men. "Well, that's the setup, boys. What do you want to do? Stick with us?"

The chorus of assents was dominated by Anderson's bass voice. "Hell, yes!"

"One more thing, gentlemen," Simon insisted. "Don't keep calling me Dr. Kirk."

"Verrra weel, me boy. Simon it is, then MacNairrr is the firrrst to declarrre it."

"Ah, *shuddup*..." Anderson rumbled.

MacNair glared balefully at his assistant as they arose to leave the mess hall. "Watch yourrr tongue, ye thick headed lout, or one of these days MacNairrr weel take offense."

Simon chuckled. In spite of himself, he liked these men.

CHAPTER SIX

THE MASTERCLOCK set high in the control room was barely past 2230 when Simon arrived from his cabin. While the ship had been circling aimlessly many miles above the North Pacific Ocean, Kirk had been studying the ship's Officer Guide and other data pertaining to the construction and operation of the vessel. His special memory training had enabled him to be as familiar with these as were the other men aboard. The technological aspects were, of course, to him, simple. It had taken more time to commit the proper commands to memory. Simon reflected that while he might not be as capable as Wingate in this matter, he was at least not useless.

He stepped to the First Officer's prescribed position in front of the intercom panel and familiarized himself with the controls, preparing to relay Wingate's landing orders. Simon connected with the Signal Officer's board.

Barronoff's sardonic face and beard appeared on the plate. "Ah, my friend, Kirk. What can I do for you?"

"Minus 90 icon. Full penetration."

"Oh ho! You've been reading the rule books, I see." Barronoff's unseen hands made several motions and his face vanished to be replaced by a blue, tinted picture of the ocean rolling on a sandy beach. The minus 90 icons in the bottom of the hull projected their searching eyes downward in full amplification, penetrating mist, haze and darkness, seeing where optical instruments detected only blackness. The scene on the plate rapidly moved inland and Kirk watched the rolling hills of sand, fascinated.

"It's unbelievable," he thought, "that once this was covered with lush green vegetations and people once worked, lived and played here." That was before the neucleatrons and the slow neutrons had done their insidious work. Early leaky atomic generators had scourged and sterilized the world, leaving a barren wasteland. Even today, the altered soils would support no plant life.

Simon glanced at the clock and cut short his reflections. He pressed the audio stud that connected him with the Navigator. "Visual coordinates on a minus 90 icon," Kirk requested.

"Yes, sir."

There was a brief pause and then hair-like lines of light seemed to attach themselves to the desert he had been observing. Each line carried a numbered designation, giving it a geographical position. As he watched, the original lines slid out of sight and new ones appeared at the top of the screen. Simon observed that they were almost over the relay station. He addressed the Navigator again. "Flight factors, please, Mr. Markham."

His reply was as expressionless as ever. "Yes, sir." After an imperceptible pause, Markham's pedantic voice began to chant the altitude, speed, drift and rate of descent, occasionally interspersed with other data.

Then something crashed into Simon's back with the impact of an avalanche, nearly sending him through the intercom panel.

"Right on the job, I see!" a booming voice deafened him. "That's the spirit!"

Kirk saw the room through a red haze. He turned on Captain Wingate like a wounded lion. "You moronic elephant! Keep your hands to yourself! What do you think I am, a punching bag? I'll break—" Kirk's rage died. "I'm sorry Captain, I didn't mean to offend—" but Wingate was beyond hearing. He clutched his stomach in an agony of mirth. His roars of laughter made loose objects in the room rattle.

SIMON STOOD by, appalled at the performance and waited for Wingate to get his breath.

Finally Wingate returned to normal. "Good boy!" he said, between gasps for air. "Got some spunk in ya after all. Knew you'd get some life into ya if ya got out from behind those books for a while."

"You're not angry?" Kirk asked.

"Hell no! Now you're talking like a man instead of a college professor. We'll make a Grade A sailor out of you yet." Wingate, still chuckling, walked to the master control panel.

"Well I'll be damned," Kirk said aloud. Strangely enough, he found himself rather pleased instead of horrified at his own conduct.

Suddenly there was no time for introspection. Wingate began the complicated and delicate landing procedure. The great hull swayed slightly as it sped downward through 18 miles of rarefied air.

Simon relayed and routed the Captain's orders as fast as he received them. He had no time now for watching; no time even for thinking. How long this went on, Simon didn't know, but just when he thought he would break under the strain, the bedlam stopped. The floor jarred slightly under his feet. They were down! Kirk's collar clung to his neck like an ancient lettuce leaf. He wiped his wet palms on his hips. Fishing in his pocket, Simon found a self-lighting cigarette.

"A little tough the first time, isn't it?" a quiet voice asked over his shoulder.

Simon turned on his heel and saw Bryant regarding him, smiling. "Huh? Oh, it's you. Yes, it was pretty tough. I don't know if I could do it again or not."

"Oh, you'll swing it all right," Bryant assured him. "You didn't make one mistake. I haven't seen a better first try in fifteen years."

They were joined by Wingate and Barronoff. Markham seemed to be busy scribbling on a report blank.

"Nice going there, sailor," Wingate boomed.

"Thanks," Kirk grinned. "I was just lucky."

"Ah, befitting modesty for the hero of the day," Barronoff remarked.

Simon was more than a little embarrassed by the attention he was receiving. Servility and subordination he was accustomed to, but admiration and appreciation from comrades was something new and a trifle discomfiting. He had never before been accepted into a group of men, particularly such a close-knit one as this, so it was not unusual that he should have some difficulty with the situation.

Markham joined the group and as usual he was all business. "We're at the coordinates as directed, sir. Shall I make a preliminary survey?"

"Are there any aircraft nearby?" the Captain asked.

"I saw none on the ground, sir, and the detectors show there are none operating in the vicinity."

"Good," Wingate replied. "Well, Simon, it's your show from now on."

KIRK HESITATED and then selected Wingate and Barronoff to accompany him on the inspection of the station.

"Just a minute, lad," Wingate suggested. "I'll get some side arms."

"Oh, I don't think that will be necessary," Simon said.

"You didn't expect to meet anyone the last time you came here but you did," Barronoff reminded him.

Kirk shrugged his shoulders. "Well, the majority rules, I guess. But we'll have to make it fast. I'd rather not be caught around here. That would make our executions a certainty."

"If we're caught anywhere," Barronoff remarked, "I assure you it is a certainty."

Simon raised his eyebrows. "You're a cheerful fellow to have around."

Wingate's voice boomed from the control room entrance. "Yes indeed, lad. You'll find that out as you get to know him better. He's had us dead and in our graves a thousand times in the last fifteen years. Why I remember once—" Wingate launched into a long tirade on one of his former exploits in which one could see that Barronoff was not the hero. The bearded man's discomfort increased with every passing minute but he said nothing.

The tirade was cut short. "Weel, weel! I see yon windbag has sprrrung anotherrr leak. And ha many heathen enemies ha ourrr noble Captain slain so farrr, me lad? Has he coom to the parrt about the wee lassie stealin' his pantaloons while the drrrunken bum slept?"

Wingate froze. No sound came from his gaping mouth. His face had the same appearance Caesar's must have had when Brutus plunged the knife into his body. MacNair enjoyed this immensely. Before the Scot could elaborate further, the Captain found his voice. "MacNair!" he brayed.

"I speak only whut is the trrruth," MacNair replied with glacial effrontery. "And I ha' in me cabin a picturrre of a cerrrtain Captain, standin' in his drrrawers, surrounded by the law. 'Tis a much youngerrrr and less repulsive Captain but there's a cerrrtain similarrrity which canna be overrrlooked."

The words hung in the air while Wingate reddened and swallowed with great difficulty. "I've got important work on my hands," he croaked, "but I'll see you later, you Scotch—!"

"Wi or wi-out yourrr trrrousers?" MacNair asked as he left the room.

Wingate made strangling noises. Barronoff burst into fresh gales of laughter as he followed. Simon could contain himself no longer and joined in the general merriment.

"I'll show you all," Wingate threatened. "You ungrateful hyenas," He twirled the unlocking wheel on the port and flung it open. Then he turned on Kirk. "And as for you...a man I thought was my friend!" Wingate's foot slipped on the freshly painted decking and he vanished through the gaping port. Simon and Barronoff rushed to the opening. The ship was perched on a hill of sand that slanted steeply away. About ten feet below them, spread-eagled on the sand, Wingate lay. "Laugh some more, ye gibbering apes!" he screamed. "Get MacNair out so he won't miss the fun! The old fool will die laughing if I've broken a leg!"

SIMON AND Barronoff dropped to the ground and tried to help Wingate rise.

"Get away from me, you fools!" Wingate roared. "I may not be young but I'm no invalid!"

Kirk was genuinely worried about him. "Are you sure you're not hurt?" he asked anxiously.

Kirk's concern seemed to please Wingate. "No lad. I'm tougher than you think. It's nice to know that somebody cares if I live or, die, though." He beamed at Simon and then scowled at Barronoff. "What about you, beanpole? Don't you care if I've broken my back or not?"

"Well, it *would* be inconvenient," Barronoff began.

Wingate's disgusted snort cut him off. "That's all I am to these village idiots," he growled. "Just a convenience. Well, come on. Let's get going so we can get out of here before someone comes along."

They walked the short distance to the small building. Kirk produced the key and opened the door. The others filed in behind him as he snapped on the light.

"Well, this is it," Simon remarked. He turned toward the huge transmitter in the center of the room. Any remarks he might have had in mind were forgotten. Standing in front of the transmitter was the same man who had been there the night before. This time, however, he had the blaster trained on Simon.

"I've been expecting you," the man said with a half smile.

"It looks as though you were expecting *somebody...*" Barronoff sneered.

"Quite right, Mr. Barronoff. We were."

Barronoff was reduced to silence. He stood dumbly, staring at the man.

"Oh yes, gentlemen," the stranger continued. "I know you all. It's really nothing to be astonished over. The world is full of free thinkers. It's not too unusual that one of them should be aboard your ship."

Wingate came of life with a roar. "A spy... A spy on my ship? Why I'll—I'll—break his back..."

The stranger continued placidly, "I'm afraid not, Captain Wingate. At least, not while this gun is pointing at you." The gun shifted slightly and centered on Wingate.

Wingate began another tirade. "Just wait...just wait till I get back. I'll grill every white-livered mother's son aboard my ship! No one is going to betray Wingate and get away with it. I swear, if it takes to my dying day, I'll keep at it and when I find out..."

As usual, Wingate was interrupted. "Ald faithful is spoutin' again I see. Regular as clockwork!"

Wingate whirled. "MacNair! You Judas!"

MacNair replied, "If ye could use yourrr eyes, you'd see me hands in the airrr! Do ya think I'd be chinnin meself at a time like this?"

"*Shuddup,*" a rumbling voice behind MacNair commanded.

MacNair snapped back. "You keep a civil tongue in yourrr head, ye grease monkey, orrr one of these days MacNairrr will lose patience."

BRYANT'S clear voice cracked a command at the two engineers.

"Line up over against that wall. You too," he snapped, indicating Barronoff and Simon. Markham entered in front of Bryant and walked over to where the others were standing.

Wingate deflated like a balloon.

"Bryant!" he said, almost sadly.

"Yes, Captain," Bryant answered. "I'm your spy."

Kirk thought he detected a mistiness in the old Captain's eyes. He realized that the affection Wingate felt for his comrades of old was not a shallow one. Bryant too seemed moved. There was much emotion in his voice when he spoke, "I'm sorry I had to do it, Captain. It wasn't easy but I believe it to be for your own good. I hope I can make you understand."

"Never…" the Captain bit out.

"I'm afraid you'll have to talk to them, Dr. Belcourt," Bryant said, softly.

Barronoff pounced on this. "So you *are* Dr. Belcourt…"

"At your service," the tall man smiled.

Kirk broke in. "What's this all about? You're supposed to be dead. Where have you been?"

Belcourt smiled again. "Why does a chicken cross the road? To get to the other side. Correspondingly, I disappeared to get to the other side."

"What other side?" Simon insisted.

"Well, there are a lot of things I can't explain to you now. What I said about that book's changing my life is literally true. I tried enlisting the aid of others so that we could form a colony somewhere and live the way we wanted to. This was done in secret of course. We looked around and found out that such a group already existed so we made arrangements and conveniently disappeared. I know our disappearance caused some comment but it appeared natural enough.

"You probably won't believe it, but our group has grown and more are coming every day. At first, all that we were interested in was seclusion so that we might live our lives as free men, but now we know that this is a selfish point of view and it's impossible. While we were a small group, everything was simple, but now that our numbers have swelled, we find concealment is oncoming more of a problem each day. Soon, at the rate we're going, we'll be discovered. If that should happen, don't think the corporations would hesitate to blast us out of existence.

"We represent a definite threat and survival is the first law of nature. Everyone is agreed that something must be done, and now, but the what of it is something else again. We don't want to be blotted out but on the other hand, we don't want to kill everyone else in order to stay alive. We need young men, geniuses if possible. Oh yes, we have lots of young people, but most of them have been raised in our colony and they don't realize the kind of odds that are against us. They are brave and their plans are good but they show a definite lack of understanding of the problem. We who are older find it hard to plan anything because of just that, our age. We know we're not going to live much longer and we're inclined to hope and pray that everything will turn out anyway.

"The Board of Governors of our group has decided upon a plan that we hope will solve our dilemma. That is why you are here, Dr. Kirk. You are the one we picked to help us.

You are experienced, a man of genius, and from you we hope to find the solution. And that is why you were lured here."

"THEN YOU deliberately created those interruptions?" Simon asked, somewhat puzzled.

"Yes," Belcourt answered. "Some years ago, I invented a simple device that I call the loader microphone. It will store up to thirty minutes' conversation, then release it at incredible speed. I attached this to your visual transmitter and sent my reports, which attracted your attention. The transmission rate is so high that no one could recognize voice patterns on the screen."

"That's something I should like to see," Simon exclaimed.

"Oh, we have lots of things that will interest you," Belcourt smiled. "I'll be glad to show them to you."

"Is that supposed to repay me for making me a hunted criminal?" Simon asked bitterly.

"I'm sorry for that," Belcourt said.

"We didn't know about Heisman's being outside until too late. When we found out about it, Roger Lourde had himself substituted for the inspector originally assigned to the job. We assisted in your escape as much as we could. George Bryant was to have followed you here but circumstances played into our hands and he came with you."

Wingate let out a roar. "Are you the ones that stole that transport?"

"Yes," Belcourt smiled, "but since it was carrying contraband, in this case guns, you would have been in more trouble than you are if we hadn't captured it. Whether you know it or not, Power City is arming in defiance of her agreements."

"How do you know?" Wingate asked.

"Oh, we have ways of finding out things," Belcourt smiled. "In our position, we have to keep up with what's going on. But I'm not much of an authority on what's going in the outside world. That's left up to a man on our Board experienced in military tactics. I think you might know him. He's General Kirk."

"*What!*" Simon was stunned. "Yes," Belcourt said gently. "Your father, Simon, is one of our Governors."

"But...but...that's impossible! My father's dead! He's been dead for thirteen years!"

The other members of the crew shifted their weight nervously.

Belcourt smiled. "He was quite alive when I left him this morning. Aren't you forgetting that I've been dead for eight years?

"But...but...the funeral?"

"You weren't there," Belcourt explained. "Don't you remember? You were away studying. Your father's somewhat peculiar will demanded immediate interment of his body and it forbade that anyone view the remains. The ones who saw the body buried were strangers to the General. As a matter of fact, the man was an old fellow officer of your father's who was staying at the house as a guest. He died of a heart attack while he was asleep and your father saw a golden opportunity to join the group of free men. It was just getting started then. So, he conveniently disappeared. The deceased had no family and few friends."

"Hmmmm. Verra interrrrrasting if trrrue!" MacNair sneered.

"GENTLEMEN, that brings me to the point of this dialogue," Belcourt added. "You'll get a chance to see whether or not I'm telling the truth because we're going to Free City. Now you can go as captives if you like. Bryant and I can spell each other watching you but it'll be difficult. On the other hand, if you will give me your paroles until we reach the city, I'll ride just as a guide. What do you want to do?"

The men looked at one another. It was plain there wasn't anything they could do.

"Well, since we'll be kidnapped in any event," Kirk suggested, "I see no reason why we shouldn't avail ourselves of your amnesty." Simon looked at Wingate. The Captain gave him a smile and nodded his head. "You have our paroles," he said.

"Thank you," Belcourt smiled. "It will be a lot easier on all of us. Now, purely as a matter of custom, gentlemen, would you deposit your weapons with Mr. Bryant on the way out?"

They filed out the doorway one by one, handing their guns to Bryant as they did so. MacNair's contribution took a little longer than the others. It included two small needle guns, an archaic forty-five-caliber automatic, a hideous knife, a blackjack and a pair of brass knuckles.

Wingate eyed the brass knuckles suspiciously. "You dirty snake!" he exploded. "You had those on that night at the Seamen's Bar! No wonder I was out for hours! Just wait! When we land again, it will be man to man and none of your dirty tricks!"

"If ye don't lose yourrr courage tween now and then, it'll be man to missing link!" MacNair bit out.

Wingate growled and gritted his teeth as they entered the ship. Simon was beginning to look forward to the long-postponed encounter with anticipation instead of anxiety.

The physical exhaustion and lack of sleep began to take their toll of Kirk. He went through the takeoff in a fog. Dr. Belcourt stood in the back of the control room, looking at the proceedings with interest. With the takeoff completed and the course set according to Belcourt's instructions, Simon began to doze at the intercom panel. He woke himself with a start. He was beginning to doze off again when MacNair entered the room.

Belcourt looked at him sharply. "I thought you were in the engine room with Bryant and Anderson."

"I was," MacNair replied innocently, "but I convinced that bonnie lad, Bryant, that the worrrd of MacNairrr is his bond. Besides, I thought I might rrrender ye a service. I stopped by me cabin and extrrracted a wee bottle of good hieland Scotch frrrom me bag."

An atmosphere of brotherly friendliness descended on Captain Wingate that was truly amazing. "MacNair, you're a true friend," he announced. "I knew you wouldn't forget your old pal, Wingate!"

MacNair regarded the Captain with a hostile stare. "Forrr ye, ya hog. I ha made a prrrominent marrrk on the bottle, doon to which level is yourrr sharrre!"

The engineer displayed the bottle. The mark was barely a sixteenth of an inch below the top of the liquid. Wingate made an inarticulate groan and snatched the bottle out of the Scot's hand. In what seemed a single motion, he opened the bottle and lowered its contents a good inch. The engineer lunged toward him, arms outstretched.

"One more step and I'll break this bottle over your penny-pinching head!" Wingate warned.

MACNAIR stopped abruptly, " 'Tis not thut I fear your puny arm but 'twould be a waste of good brrrew. Therrre will be no bloodshed if ye gi' it back!"

Wingate acceded to his demand and the Scot passed the bottle around to the others although a trifle grudgingly. Barronoff and Markham accepted but Belcourt declined, smiling. Kirk too would have refused but MacNair urged him.

"Coom lad! Twill do ye a worrrld of good."

Simon was too tired to argue. The liquor was warming and in a moment new strength seemed to flow into his tired limbs. The Chief Engineer drank deeply and handed the bottle again to Kirk. This time he didn't try to refuse. "This is good," Simon commented.

"Naturrrally," the old Scot replied. "The whiskey of the hielands was made forrr discrrrriminating gentlemen."

MacNair took another gulp and returned the bottle to Kirk. Wingate watched hungrily but knew the Scotchman was too canny to be caught off guard again. In a surprisingly short time the bottle was empty. MacNair studied it ruefully then tossed it to Wingate. "Herrre, ye glutton! What is left I freely gi' to ye."

Wingate caught the bottle expertly and scrutinized it preparatory to draining the last few drops. Then he let out a roar that shook the walls, "You filthy Scotchman! You took this from *my* cabin!"

MacNair passed through the door an instant before the bottle crashed into a million fragments on its edge. Kirk noted with illogical amusement that Belcourt had drawn his gun. With an animal sound Wingate turned his back on the doorway and Belcourt relaxed.

Simon laughed aloud. The others joined him with the exception of Markham, who seldom laughed at anything. Kirk reeled a little unsteadily and would have fallen had he not grasped the hand rail beside him. Even at that, he had some trouble getting back to his feet.

Barronoff studied Simon closely. "You'd better take it easy, boy," he warned. "You've had one too many."

"That's a matter of opinion," Kirk asserted. "I can take care of myself…"

"You'd better sit down just the same," Barronoff insisted.

"Lishon goat face! I'm—I'm perfffly capable of stttandin on my ffeet if I feel like it," Simon replied belligerently. To illustrate this, he staggered back a few steps to recover his balance. "Quit tiltin the shipppp!" Kirk ordered. "Wh—what ya tryin to do? Knock me downnnn?"

Wingate's bellows of laughter infuriated Simon beyond endurance. His gaze settled on Barronoff. "YOU did it!" he accused thickly. Suiting action to the word, he launched a vicious right straight for Barronoff's black beard but Barronoff's head moved and the fist went on, unresisted. Simon was thrown off balance and fell headlong into Barronoff's arms. Somehow Kirk didn't have the strength to get back on his feet again and, after a brief struggle, he relaxed limply and closed his eyes.

"Lemme go," Simon muttered feebly.

Barronoff's body shook so hard with laughter that he could hardly hold Simon up. The shaking must have been soothing to Kirk for presently he began to snore.

Belcourt's laughter died away to a chuckle. "I think one of you better put him to bed."

Barronoff lifted Kirk up into his arms and carried him like a baby down the companionway.

CHAPTER SEVEN

THE FIRST sensation that Simon felt on awakening was that of a deliciously cold hand stroking his forehead gently. The second was that of a horrible nausea. To this was added a pounding headache as though someone was beating on his skull with a sledge hammer. Simon opened his eyes to see the owner of the cool hand, but even the dim light of his cabin was intolerable.

A musical, feminine voice enticed him. "Are you awake?"

Simon nodded.

"Here," she said. "Sit up and take these. They'll make you feel better."

The girl helped him sit up and placed two pearly white capsules in his hand. Kirk popped them into his mouth and groped blindly for a glass of water. The pills went down with the ease of two baseballs. The urge to gag left Simon but he felt weaker than before. He eased himself back against the pillows, groaning.

"Oh my gawd! I hope those pills were poison!"

Soon the headache disappeared and the will to die was gone. Simon opened his eyes again and, at a glance, he could see he was still in his own cabin. A girl with flowing blonde hair was seated beside the bunk. She was dressed in a summery white blouse and knee-length blue skirt. She was very beautiful to Simon. Then he suddenly discovered that, except for the blanket over him, he was completely without clothes.

"You didn't—" he began, reddening. "That is, I mean—"

She seemed to divine his thoughts. "No. Ivan Barronoff put you to bed. I've only been here a few minutes."

Kirk's sigh was audible. The girl smiled. Suddenly Simon frowned and looked intently at her. "I've seen you somewhere before."

The girl's laugh tinkled in the room. "That line is as old as the hills. You'll have to think of something better than that."

Simon blushed. "Oh no! I certainly didn't mean—that is, it's not a—"

"I know. I'm sorry," she apologized. "You saw me yesterday at the information desk in the Cominc building."

Kirk digested this for a moment then asked, "Where are we now?"

"The ship is in the hangar of Free City," she answered.

"Is that so?" Simon retorted. "And I suppose you have a dozen armed guards outside the door."

The girl bit her lip. "That remark wasn't very worthy of you."

Kirk felt ashamed. "I'm sorry."

Her bright smile warmed him again.

"Oh that's all right. I guess you don't feel too well yet."

KIRK ADMITTED there had been times when he had felt better. "By the way," he asked, "where is the rest of the crew?"

"Oh, they left hours ago," the girl explained. "Mr. Bryant is showing them the city."

"So they deserted me, eh?" Simon smiled.

"Do you think I could substitute for them for a while?" the girl inquired.

Kirk was slightly embarrassed. "Of course. I mean—ah, if—you want to."

"Do you think you could stand a bite to eat now?" she asked solicitously.

"Indeed I could," Kirk answered.

"Good," she smiled. "There's a little restaurant just outside the field. I'll wait outside while you dress."

She arose, nodded and closed the door softly behind her. Kirk dressed rapidly and made himself as presentable as possible. In a few minutes he stepped outside and joined the girl.

"Well, do you think I'll pass, Miss—ah?"

"Belcourt," she supplied, "but just call me Ellen."

"Belcourt?" Simon echoed.

"Dr. Belcourt is my father," she answered.

"Well, well, quite a family affair, isn't it," he muttered.

She replied, "Your family is well represented too, Dr. Kirk. Your father is on the Board of Governors!"

"I'd like to see him as soon as possible. At least, I'll find out for sure if he is my father."

"You're not going anywhere," she ordered, "until you've had breakfast…"

"Since I don't know my way around," Simon replied, "I'm afraid I'm in your clutches."

She lifted her eyebrows. "Is it that bad?"

Kirk colored. "I didn't mean that the way it sounded."

She laughed and Simon chimed in. Just then they reached the hangar exit.

"Nice field you have here," Kirk commented. The field was small but well built. There were only two hangars, the large one from which they had emerged and a smaller one on the other side of the Administration Building. Surrounding the building was a well-kept lawn and garden.

"I'm glad you like our field," she replied. "The garden was my idea. The Governors couldn't see it at first but I convinced them."

"I like gardens too," Simon said impulsively.

"My…you're just full of surprises Dr. Kirk," she replied.

"I—I'd rather you didn't keep on calling me Dr. Kirk," Simon said. "It sounds so formal."

"What'll it be then? Simon?" she questioned.

"If you don't mind," he agreed diffidently.

"I don't at all. I think it's a nice name." She turned. "Here's the restaurant I spoke about."

As they entered, Simon noted at once the paintings on the walls.

"Almost every newcomer stops here to eat," Ellen explained, "so the walls are decorated with murals showing the progress of Free City."

Kirk noticed them with interest. "They're very well done."

"Yes. They were made by an old man who escaped from a Fabrinc prison." Her forefinger pointed to one of the first murals. "He was sentenced to prison for life for painting that face."

IT WAS A picture of a ruddy-faced man with a wiry gray mustache. He was in old-fashioned dress and wearing quaint gold-rimmed spectacles. Immediately below the portrait was painted a large representation of a club or heavy stock.

Simon's blank expression betrayed him.

"You don't know who that is, do you?" Ellen asked with a trace of bitterness.

Simon shook his head.

"He was the twenty-fifth president of the old United States, Theodore Roosevelt. That thing below him is the big stick he used on businesses that got too big and tried to run people's lives. If there were a few men like him in the world today, no corporation would put people in prisons or execute them. In those days they couldn't put you in jail for painting a picture, writing a book, or saying what you thought."

"Well, someone has to keep order," Simon argued. "I don't see that it makes much difference who does it."

Ellen's eyes blazed slightly. "It doesn't matter whether or not some stranger tells you how to live your life? Or whether you decide for yourself...?"

"Well, you can't live your life without regard for the people around you."

"Did the Director General of your corporation have so much concern for the people around him when he had those three Directors executed? All they wanted to do was elect a new president..."

"According to the company law, that's treason. They should have been executed and *they were...*"

"Oh, you make me sick!" she flared.

They finished their meal in uncomfortable silence.

Kirk finally spoke. "I didn't mean to offend you. I'm afraid I'm always saying the wrong thing to you."

"Oh, it isn't your fault," she replied contritely. "It's just that the topic is one of my sore spots. I try very hard to control my temper but it gets the best of me sometimes."

For some reason, Simon felt greatly relieved. "I finished my breakfast as you insisted," he said, laughing.

"All right," she replied. "I'll take you to your father."

When they reached the walk in front of the restaurant, Simon stopped suddenly. "Say..." he exclaimed. "We forgot to pay for our breakfast. I have lots of credits. Are they good here?"

"Pay?" she retorted, laughing. "We don't have to pay for anything!"

"Oh, because of your father," he said.

"Of course not. We don't have any monetary system," Ellen explained.

"You mean, you—you just help yourself—to anything you want?" Kirk asked incredulously. "Everybody does?"

"Certainly. It's everybody's property."

"Well—who does the work? I mean, well—doesn't everyone sit around and let things go?"

ELLEN TRIED to explain as patiently as a mother would to a child. "Simon, everything in this city belongs to me and to everyone else who lives here. Unlike most of the citizens, I haven't stuck to any one job. I've drifted here and there doing what is needed doing at the time."

Simon turned this over in his mind carefully. "Are you given this freedom because of your position?" he asked.

"What position? I haven't any position. All the citizens are free to do as they please."

Kirk shook his head. "I don't quite understand it," he said. "You must have a very high type of individual here. I know if I were unrestricted that I might do some work, mostly to keep from getting bored, but I certainly wouldn't work more than a day or possibly two at the most in a week's time."

"A day's work is twice as much as the average citizen does in a week," Ellen informed him.

"Only half a day a week! How do you keep the place going?"

"Oh it's really quite simple. Ninety percent of the work is done by machinery. Atomic power supplies the effort. If we had a monetary system, there would be almost eight hours of work for every able-bodied man and woman each week."

"I don't see what a monetary system has to do with it," Kirk answered.

"Well, suppose you were working in a bank or in a payroll department," Ellen explained. "You would work for a salary. You'd eat just as much and require just as much clothing as anybody else but you wouldn't help to make the clothing or grow the food."

"Yes—" Simon admitted, "but we've always found that bankers and accountants were essential."

"Furthermore," she pointed out, "unless you owned the business, someone would be making a profit on the work that you do. You won't believe me when I tell you that with all the facilities our civilization has to offer, you would only have to contribute a little over half an hour a day to be entirely self-supporting."

"It doesn't seem possible," Simon murmured.

"I'm no authority," Ellen said, "but our production coordinator can show you all the facts and figures. The only thing I know is that it works."

Simon had to admit that the existence of the city was some proof of her statements but he could look into details later. At this point, they reached a tastefully landscaped park and they stopped by a bench. They sat down as though by mutual consent.

"As I see it," Simon said thoughtfully, "it's a very attractive proposition. All a person has to do is work about four hours a week or whatever your conscience tells you to and the rest of the time you can spend doing whatever you want to, like—oh, panting pictures or—writing—or learning to play the piano."

Ellen laughed. "I'm afraid not," she replied. "Such things are considered just as much of a contribution as tending a water-purifying plant or a textile machine."

"But that's a contradiction of what you were saying a moment ago," Simon protested.

"Is it?" she asked. "There's a book that's still a best seller even after a few thousand years. In it, it says that man cannot live by bread alone. There are many people that can't live without good music, good books or even an occasional glimpse of a masterful painting. That is why there is always an over-supply of labor."

SIMON WAS confused. "But don't too many people try to become artists or something?"

"Do you want to become an artist?" Ellen asked.

"Well, no. But that's different," Simon protested.

"Oh, no, it isn't!" Ellen replied. "The world is literally overflowing with technicians and experts but we haven't half enough authors, musicians, composers and the like."

"Maybe so," Simon commented.

The girl looked at her tiny watch set in a finger ring. "My, it's 1300 already. Your father will be chewing his nails off!"

Kirk was ashamed of himself. During this engrossing discussion, he had forgotten completely about his father.

"Come along. Simon. We've got to prove some things to you," Ellen called gaily as she led the way down the path. She began to run. "I'll race you to the street!"

Kirk raced to catch her and overtook her before they reached the street. He caught her arm and spun her around. "I may be advanced in age but I'm well preserved!" he said between gasps. "Clean living and exercise…"

They stood then, face to face, breathing rapidly and laughing. Ellen's eyes sparkled and her cheeks were flushed. Simon's heart thudded strangely for so slight an exertion. For just an instant, he felt a trifle dizzy.

"Ellen," he said in an unusually intense voice.

"Yes Simon?" she said, softly.

"Ah…nothing." He paused. "Is my father's house nearby?"

"It's not too far from here," she replied quietly, "but he won't be home now. He's waiting for us at his office. We'd better take a taxi."

Kirk was puzzled. Ellen seemed disappointed or displeased at something. "I must have said something to offend her," he thought. "I'll have to watch myself."

They found a taxi parked nearby and climbed in. A few minutes later they drew to a stop in front of a tall, imposing white building.

"This is it." Ellen remarked. She seemed to have recovered her good spirits. Simon followed her inside and into the elevator.

"This is a little different type from the ones you're used to," she commented.

Kirk noted at once the absence of the usual gravity neutralizer.

Ellen turned her face to a small panel in the wall. "Twenty-three," she ordered.

"Twenty-three," a metallic voice replied.

"I never have gotten used to having a machine talk back to me," Ellen laughed.

The lift raced upwards with an amazing speed and came to a smooth stop before a door. It opened automatically and they stepped out into a large, well-furnished room. There was a blond young man sitting behind a desk in one corner. He looked up from his work. "Hello, Ellen!"

"Hello, Jeff!" she responded brightly, too brightly, Simon thought. "I want you to meet the famous Dr. Simon B. Kirk Simon, this is Jeffrey Davis."

JEFF'S HAND was firm and enthusiastic. "Please to meet you, Dr. Kirk. I've heard a lot about you, mostly from Ellen."

Ellen blushed furiously and hastily changed the subject. "Is the General in?"

"He sure is!" Jeff grinned. "He's been waiting on pins and needles all morning. Go right in."

Ellen led Simon through a large, walnut doorway. Seated at the far end of the room was a man who looked like an older edition of Kirk himself, tall, bronzed and athletic. His white hair held the same suggestion of wave as did Simon's. He got to his feet as Kirk came toward the desk, slowly. The old man's voice was husky with emotion. "Simon. It's so good to see you."

Simon's eyes were misty. There was no longer any doubt. "Dad."

They embraced each other silently for a moment. Then they stood back and looked at each other intently.

"You haven't changed much, dad," Kirk said softly.

"You sure have, son. My, but you've filled out. I've always thought of you as being a beanpole. How much do you weigh now?"

Simon didn't get a chance to answer. A small sound made both men turn and look at Ellen. Tears were streaming down her face but she was smiling. She ineffectually tried to wipe them away with the back of her hand. Simon's father drew a large handkerchief from his pocket.

"There, there, child," the General said, soothingly. "There's nothing to cry about. You ought to be happy. Haven't you been after me for over a year to bring him here?"

Ellen hid her crimson face in the folds of the handkerchief. "Well, the city can use men like him," she stammered in a muffled voice.

"That's right," the General said, stroking her head.

"Dad," Kirk broke in, "why didn't you let me know where you were? Why did you let me think you were dead?"

"Well son, I couldn't help it. If the companies had found out about this place, they would have blown it out of existence."

Simon was hurt. "But you know I'd never betray you!"

"I know, son," the old man replied. "At least not consciously. But it's just like you to try to rescue me, to save me from myself—as it were."

Simon looked at him blankly and nodded his head. "Yes, that's just what I would have tried to do."

Father and son talked for some time about the old days. There was much to say on both sides but it would take days, maybe even weeks before they could exhaust everything. Finally the General turned to Ellen. "Why don't you take this son of mine out and show him the rest of the city?"

"But Dad!" Simon protested. "I've got so many things—"

"I know, I know, but you can ask them at dinner tonight," his father answered. "I've got work to do. Why don't you meet me here about 1700. Ellen can show you the city and save me a lot of trouble answering questions. Take my word for it, Simon, she's a regular Baedeker."

"A what?" Simon asked.

"You tell him, Ellen," the General laughed. "Now take your hero out and show him the town."

ELLEN ushered Simon out of the office with more haste than necessary, Simon thought. When they finally reached the street, he stopped her firmly. "Now look here, young lady. There's something I want to know..."

Ellen avoided his gaze. "Yes?"

"What is a Baedeker?"

"Oh," she answered with obvious relief. "It was an old official guide to large cities." She lapsed into silence and kept her eyes averted.

Simon was silent too. I've offended her again, he thought. The feminine mind had always been a puzzle to him. Maybe if I can think of something funny to say, she'll be all right.

Ellen turned suddenly. "Let's not stand in the doorway," she suggested. "Come on and I'll show you our city."

He assented and they climbed into a taxi. Ellen was herself again and Simon again was relieved. He saw all the points of interest and major attractions. He saw vegetables growing in chemical solution, visited the synthetic proteins plant and such like. An amazing number of the plants were automatic.

Mid point in their journey, Simon paused to ask why such a large city had never been discovered by the outside world.

"I should let my father explain it to you," she answered. "He's the chief of Scientific Works. When the city was first started and numbered only a few houses, your father camouflaged it with wire netting and artificial trees. By the time my father arrived, the city was almost too large to be concealed. He and some other men set to work and built a third-dimensional image projector, sort of a televisor that needs no receiver. This projects an image that covers the city entirely. All you can see from the air is a barren, volcanic island with no trees and no place to land anything but a helicopter. Only one exploring party has ever tried to land. And were they surprised to see our men coming out of a solid rock mountain!"

Simon looked up. "I don't see anything, just a little haze."

"That's it," Ellen said. "It shows no image this way, but it looks real enough on the other side."

Kirk made a mental note to ask Ellen's father about the technical details. This was in his field and he had never heard or seen anything like it.

The journey finally ended in a wing of the Archives Building. Ellen led him to a large glass case behind which was a very weathered document.

"One of our ancestors signed that," she commented. Kirk couldn't make out the writing. A transcription was fastened to the surface of the glass case. Ellen's finger pointed to a passage.

" 'We hold these truths to be self evident,' " Simon read slowly, " 'that all men are created equal...' "

Ellen stood patiently while Simon read it through to the end. When he had finished, she waited for him to say something.

"Very interesting," he commented.

ELLEN SIGHED. "Simon, do you know what *they* meant and what *we* mean when we say life, liberty and the pursuit of happiness?"

Simon looked embarrassed. "I think so."

"Are you sure?" Ellen replied. "Did your corporation derive its powers from the consent of the governed?"

He said nothing.

"Do you know what is meant when someone says that freedom is your *right* and that anyone who tries to take it away from you is wrong?"

Simon kept his eyes on the transcript. This was confusing to him.

"You don't have to take my word for it," Ellen continued. "Look over here." They walked to the next glass case. "Here's the old Constitution of the United States and the first ten amendments are to protect the people's freedoms."

Simon decided to read it through to the end. When he had finished, they moved to the next case.

"This is a copy of the Atlantic Charter. This was supposed to keep people from being enslaved anywhere in the world." Ellen stopped abruptly.

"You feel pretty strongly about this, don't you?" Simon asked.

Ellen was solemn. "I don't know if you can understand what I'm trying to say," Ellen said softly, "but we believe that while there is even one slave in the world, no one can really be free. The men who wrote these documents were a lot older and a lot wiser than I am, but they realized it too. They didn't write all these things just to use up paper. They didn't do it either because they wanted to feel important. They believed in what they wrote. History proved that. And I believe in it too." She pointed to another smaller glass case. "This is Abraham Lincoln's Gettysburg Address. He led the United States into a war just to keep the spirit of the Constitution you read. He freed the slaves yet they shot him for what he believed in. Do you think he would have given up his ideals even if he had known that it was going to cost him his life? I know they don't teach you these things in the company schools. They only teach you what they want you to know. They picture Lincoln as a dreamer, Washington as a blundering fool who was just lucky and Franklin Roosevelt as a weakling."

Simon nodded. That's just exactly what they taught.

"I wonder, Simon," Ellen said speculatively. "Do you think these men were fools? Do you think they were fools for living, working and sometimes, dying for an ideal? Do you think we're fools for wanting to live as men instead of as animals?" Her voice died away in echoes. Then she added softly, "Do you think our fathers are fools too?"

Perplexed, Simon stumbled for an answer. "No—I don't think they're fools but—I haven't thought much about it." Kirk was more profoundly stirred than he dared admit. He looked back at the musty parchment and reread the words, 'life, liberty and the pursuit of happiness.' They were strangely inspiring. These were the things his father had left a good position for; had let his only son think he was dead for. Slowly the meaning of the words began to form in his mind and he looked at Ellen as though seeing and yet not seeing. "I—I think I know what they meant," he said simply, "but I—I never knew that—"

"I know," Ellen said quickly. "It's all new to you and you find it hard to understand just what it's all about. There are many things here that will be new and strange to you, Simon, but if you'll take the time to read and study and find out what we're trying to accomplish. I'm sure you'll find it worth the time…"

SIMON NODDED. "I'd like to do that."

"You see," Ellen continued, "that's the reason why you were brought here. Your father didn't want to have you kidnapped, but how else would you have come? He wants you to stay here and help us. We need someone like you, someone who has a good grasp of things. Your father has a lot of faith in you, Simon, and he's so sure you'll want to stay. The important thing, though, is not to make a hasty decision. Don't say no to your father until you've had a chance to really understand all this, and then, if you still don't believe in what we're doing, a way can be made to send you back. What do you say, Simon? Will you give us a try?"

Simon laughed. "This is really ridiculous! I couldn't go back even if I wanted to. Look at the mess I left things in!"

"That could be fixed up all right. In fact, you could go back a hero if you wanted to," Ellen said sadly, "but we're hoping you won't want to."

The expression on Kirk's face became grave. "I don't know what I want to do, actually. One thing I do know is that I won't make any kind of decision until I know just what I'm doing."

Ellen smiled. "Well, that's all anyone can ask, really. I just hope you'll come to be one of us here in Free City. We— we—" Ellen's voice trailed off into silence. She looked away suddenly. "I'd like you to stay."

Unaccountably there was a lump in Simon's throat. "I'll stay," he said simply.

They looked at each other and smiled.

CHAPTER EIGHT

DINNER WAS over and a lull had been reached in the conversation. They were still seated around the table, General Kirk at one end and Dr. Belcourt at the other, Simon sat on his father's right. Next to him was Ellen, then MacNair and Bryant. Ranged along the other side were Wingate, Markham, Anderson and Barronoff. Most of the men were drinking some very excellent brandy. Throughout dinner, Dr. Belcourt had given everyone a comprehensive and humorous history of Free City. The General passed cigars around.

MacNair sniffed the fragrant tobacco. "Considerrrably betterrr quality than the ald skin-flint Captain smokes," he observed in a loud voice to no one in particular.

A purple tide coursed up Wingate's neck. "Nice layout you have here," he said to the General in a strained voice.

"Glad you like it," the General chuckled. "We're rather proud of it ourselves."

"My Chief Engineer," Wingate said in an undertone that could be heard on the street outside, "is a rather dishonest fellow. I'd watch the silverware if I were you."

MacNair's stage whisper to Belcourt was plainly audible to all. "If ye will, humorrr yon Captain. He's just a wee bit daft. Ald age, ye know."

Ellen looked at Simon apprehensively.

"This goes on all the time," he said, grinning.

The General cleared his throat. "Gentlemen, and you too, my dear," nodding to Ellen, "if you don't mind, I have a few things I'd like to say."

The room became quiet.

"Mr. Bryant took you men on a group tour of our city today and you had a chance to see the city in operation. We have gone to a great deal of trouble to bring you here. Our primary purpose was to bring my son but I assure you other gentlemen that you are not unwelcome. What we can offer you here has some disadvantages but I think the advantages far outweigh them. Now, even though I know it's short notice, we would like to know if you would like to remain here. I think you've seen enough to decide but, before you answer, I must explain the other side of the question. Our psychologists can remove your recent memories and by suggestion substitute others. The missing cargo liner, which created Captain Wingate's dilemma, is here. The crew has elected to remain here but we could damage the hull and place it on some remote island. With your artificially implanted memories, you would actually believe that you had found it there and could return to your city without fear of retribution. Any connection between you and my son was taken care of back in Transinc so you would have nothing to fear there. In effect, I am offering you either choice without any artificial disadvantages so that you can make your decision without the pressure of expediency." The General paused. "Are there any questions?"

WINGATE looked at Simon. "What about you, lad? What are you going to do?"

Ellen interrupted. "Oh, he's going to stay. He decided this afternoon."

Barronoff gave Simon a significant raised eyebrow. "This afternoon?" Barronoff repeated with rising inflection.

"Yes, this afternoon," Kirk replied somewhat stiffly. "Is there anything wrong in that?"

"Now, now, don't get mad at Uncle Ivan. Remember what happened the last time you tried that."

Laughter ran around the table and Simon glanced uncomfortably at his father. The General smiled and said, "Gentlemen, there's something I forgot to mention. The whole group needn't decide as one. We can find a satisfactory situation so that we could return one or more if you decided to split the group."

There was silence for a moment while the men sat staring at various objects in the room. No one seemed to want to be the first to speak. Finally, MacNair stood up. He nodded his head toward Wingate. "In spite of the fact that yon windbag wull say 'tis because everrrything is frrree, I has decided to stay."

Wingate followed with, "Why he'd live in hell if they served free beer. Nail down the silverware, boys! MacNair is staying."

"Shuddup!" Anderson boomed, and strangely enough. Wingate did.

More quietly, Captain Wingate said, "If MacNair is going to stay, I feel it's my duty to stay too."

Barronoff arose. "For my part, I believe I shall remain."

The room became silent again. Everyone waited as though wondering who would speak next. The General was about to say something when the blond giant Anderson stood up.

"General Kirk," he said in his deep voice. "I have always lived a solitary life. About the only friends I've ever had are these shipmates of mine. I have absolutely nothing to return to but it is not because of this that I would like to stay. I've always dreamed of a place like this, a place where a man could call his life his own. The only thing I'm sorry about is that I didn't know about this city years ago. If I may, I should like to stay."

Barronoff gasped. MacNair's aplomb was shattered. "Neverrr in fifteen yearrrs ha he said so much!" he said, almost in a whisper.

Wingate was limited to an incredulous, soft, "My gawd!"

The members of the crew stared at Anderson as though seeing him for the first time.

MARKHAM looked at the General. "I'll make it unanimous, sir," he said quietly.

The General smiled. "Thank you, gentlemen. I know you won't regret your decision. And now on behalf of the citizens of Free City let me welcome you. I hope you will be happy here. You men are the type that any community would be proud to have among its members. If ever there is anything that you don't understand about the city or anything pertaining to it, please feel free to ask me or any Board member about it. Now gentlemen, I know you will be wanting to settle yourselves in your quarters so I'll cut our discussion short. I'll see that your belongings are moved over here from the ship and Mr. Bryant can show you your accommodations."

The men stood up and walked leisurely toward the door. Wingate linked arms with Bryant. "Why didn't you tell us about this place before?" he growled. "Holding out on your old pals like this…"

" 'Tis typical of the ald windbag," MacNair commented to the General. "When ye gi' him something frrree, he wants ta know why ye ha' not done so yearrrs beforrre."

"Now listen here, MacNair…" The voices became indistinguishable as the door closed.

"Well, I guess we'd better be going, too, eh, Ellen?" Dr. Belcourt suggested.

"I suppose so," she agreed half-heartedly.

Simon and his father saw them to the door. Dr. Belcourt and the General seemed to be paying a great deal of attention to the skyline of the city while Kirk said goodnight to Ellen. "I'll see you tomorrow, I hope," he said softly.

She nodded her head. "I'll be at the laboratory. Come up if you get the chance."

For some reason, Simon took Ellen's hand and squeezed it reassuringly. He dropped it immediately and wondered why he had done it. Ellen just stared down the street. Then she turned and smiled. "Good night," she whispered.

"Good night," Simon answered.

He watched Ellen and Dr. Belcourt walk down the street and then stepped back inside. He sighed and looked at his father. "What a day."

The General smiled. "It sure has been, son. Say, I've been hearing rumors about you. It seems that you—ah— were a little under the weather yesterday. Are you going to turn playboy at this late date?"

"Yes, I think so too," Simon said absently as he looked out a window.

"Simon!" the General laughed. "You haven't heard a word I've said."

"Why of course I have, Dad."

"Maybe, but I doubt it."

Simon gave him a puzzled look.

"Oh, come along," his father said. "I'll show you to your room and then you can daydream to your heart's content."

They walked down the hall. After Simon closed his door, the General stood outside smiling. Then he shook his head, still smiling and went into his own room.

CHAPTER NINE

THE SUCCEEDING days were busy ones for Kirk. He found the city and everything in it fascinating. He went through all the plants, studied methods, asked questions, even stopped people on the street and talked to them. He went often to the Archives Building and read volumes of material. His favorite spot was The Scientific Laboratory, of which Dr. Belcourt was the head. He liked to watch Dr. Belcourt at work on his inventions and tried to help him as much as he could. This also gave him a chance to see Ellen since she spent much of her time with her father.

Simon decided that the laboratory was the place he wanted to work in so he did. He had much to learn but it wasn't long before he knew the principles of almost all of the new inventions that had been turned out at the Scientific Laboratory. Besides working, Simon did a lot of thinking, so much so that sometimes Simon's father accused him of daydreaming.

One evening at dinner, Kirk aired his feelings. Dr. Belcourt and Ellen were there as they often were, but Kirk felt impelled to say something.

"Dad," he said thoughtfully, "when I first came here I agreed to stay long enough to find out all about Free City and then make a decision as to whether or not to continue to stay here. Well, I've made my decision."

Ellen looked puzzled. Simon's father was disturbed.

"I'm willing to stay, but on one condition." Simon paused and looked at his father. "I think you know what it is, Dad."

The General shook his head. "I don't think so, son."

"Well, it's this. I insist that we do something about the rest of the world." No one spoke. They didn't seem to understand him. "I mean, we've got to give back the boon of liberty to the rest of the world."

The General sighed. "That's easier said than done. You'd better explain, son. Maybe we could understand you better."

"Well, I admit I've been converted as completely as a man can be converted. I feel as though I've come to life—or—been awakened from a deep sleep. I know what it's like to talk and deal with men as friends and comrades instead of subordinates or superiors. For the first time in my life I'm doing what I want to do without worrying about anything. This is paradise, but it's paradise with a string attached. You've been gone from the outside world a long time but I still remember it well. I remember what life was like, what the average day was like, and I can't forget all those people back there, living out their lives as slaves and they *don't even know it!* They don't know any better. And there's no one to teach them that they don't have to be slaves."

Simon looked at Ellen and the light in her eyes bespoke something more than admiration. Kirk's voice rang with a new confidence. "What I want to do is convince the people and the Board of Governors to come out of hiding and help the rest of the world. I have some ideas on how it can be done. We'll have to start in a small way, of course, but I implore you that it must be done. It's my firm belief that we can't maintain our liberty by hiding it or isolating it. Sooner or later the forces of oppression and tyranny will discover it and crush it. Liberty and slavery cannot exist side by side in peace."

DR. BELCOURT smiled as he recognized the quotation from Simon Bolivar. Kirk's voice was quieter now. "If I can't convince anyone, if the Board of Governors insist upon isolation, then I ask that I be allowed to go back to the outside world. I'll have to work alone that way but if I have to, I will. You know I'll never reveal the existence of the city. All I ask is a chance, a chance to help the world, and if you won't help me; then I'll do it by myself..."

Pride and admiration made the General's voice a little unsteady as he spoke to his son. "Son, I can only say more power to you. You—you have surprised me a little. You know your views are not novel. They weren't even unique when Thomas Jefferson framed the Declaration of Independence. I think these ideas are older than history, yet they have always been and still are a young man's ideas. This city has profited by the example of history. It's been proved time and time again that freedom can only be won by young men. The Board of Governors, myself included, are advanced in years but we are young enough in spirit to know that younger, fresher minds must build the future world. The people agree and they have asked for young, vigorous leadership but they also want to retain our more experienced judgment. The present Board members have retained their seats by popular consent almost since the founding of the city. You see, son, the people who have come here were not the leaders of the outside world. The leaders of the outside world achieved a measure of satisfaction in their life just as you yourself did, Simon."

The General paused, thoughtfully. "Simon, a vacancy exists on the Board and this is to be filled by appointment, subject to the consent of the people. Some of the younger groups insist that this vacancy be filled by a man of known leadership and ability, brought in from the outside. Of all the names suggested, yours received the highest vote and so you were brought here. If you feel that you can accept this responsibility, I can offer this position to you providing the other members of the Board find you acceptable. I don't promise that we'll follow you in everything you might want to do...but together we might evolve a plan for freeing the world. At least we can try. Would you like to do that?"

Simon hesitated noticeably. Ellen urged him on. "Go on, Simon. Of course you can do it."

"Well," Simon replied, "I'll tell the Board exactly what I think should be done. My position will depend on what they decide about my plans. If they like them, fine. If they don't, then I insist on returning."

Dr. Belcourt smiled. "We'll listen to you, Simon, and if you are as convincing before the Board as you are tonight, I don't think you have a thing to worry about."

"When do we see the Board?" Simon asked.

"At 1000 tomorrow," the General said, "but we can put it off for a few days if you'd like."

"No," Simon answered. "Tomorrow is it. It can't be too soon. I want to get started."

"Edward, suppose you bring out some of that good brandy of yours," Dr. Belcourt suggested. "I'd like to drink a toast to our new Governor!"

THE GENERAL smiled. "Sometimes your ideas are excellent, Art."

Just as the General was opening a decanter of brandy, there was a knock at the door. "Come in," the General called.

The lean face of MacNair was the first to appear through the doorway. He was followed by his five comrades.

"We dinna like ta intrrrude, Generrral, but Mr. Bryant ha' preparrred us quarrrters nearrr the airrr field and we werrre anxious to move as quickly as possible. Not thut we dinna apprrrreciate yourrr hospitality but the atmosphere arrrround an airrr terminal is conducive to quiet thought."

Simon had an immediate flash of what MacNair meant by 'quiet thought.'

"Certainly, gentlemen," the General responded heartily, "but before you go, won't you have a glass of brandy?"

"Weel—aye. Thut we weel!"

"Dr. Belcourt," Simon said conversationally, "have you noticed the magnetic attraction between an open bottle and Mr. MacNair? It should prove quite interesting for laboratory study."

MacNair stared at Simon over the rim of his glass. "I seem to remember, an experrriment of thut magnetic attrrraction of which ye speak. I thought it verra instrrructive, didn't ye, Dr. Kirk?"

"Be careful what you say," Dr. Belcourt warned. "Dr. Kirk will be on the Board of Governors tomorrow."

Barronoff looked surprised. "Well," he said, shrugging, "I suppose I should congratulate you, although I would have been a better man for the job."

"Shuddup!" Anderson boomed. Since his earlier speech he had reverted to his use of monosyllabics.

Wingate practically charged across the room.

Simon hastily set his glass down in preparation of what was to come. He was pummeled, beaten and shaken. Wingate's bellowed congratulations left Simon almost deaf. Finally, Wingate was forced aside by MacNair. "Dinna monopolize the hand of a grrreat man."

Wingate relinquished the hand and the Scotchman gripped it like a vise. "Kirk is a good Scotch name, me lad. Ya weel go far."

Kirk breathed easier when the giant, Anderson passed by with a laconic "Congratulations." The grip of his ham-like hands had been consciously restrained.

Barronoff quietly said, "If there's a good position open and you need a competent executive, I'm sure you won't forget your old friend."

"If they had jails, you crook," Simon replied, laughing, "I'd throw you in for life."

When Simon finally managed to escape from the spotlight, he found that Ellen had gone and unobtrusively left the room. At the front door he almost ran over Jeff Davis.

"This is the second time I've almost been run down on this doorstep," Jeff exclaimed. "The place is definitely unsafe."

"Oh?" Simon said, trying to think of some excuse for leaving him there.

"Yes," Jeff continued. "Ellen almost ran over me a few minutes ago. I just saw her home. Is the General in?"

"Yes he is. Go on in. He's in the study."

"Thanks," Jeff said and disappeared rather hurriedly down the hall.

SIMON WALKED briskly down the street to the Belcourt residence. He hesitated a moment, then pressed the button. A few minutes passed. He listened but Simon couldn't hear any sound within the house. He pressed the button again, longer this time. Still no answer. Simon finally walked dejected down the steps. The street seemed empty and unfriendly. Even the soft night breeze seemed cooler, less pleasant. Simon was approaching his father's house when Jeff emerged. Simon purposely paused. He was in no mood to talk to anyone.

Jeff walked quickly to a taxi parked at the curb. The door opened as he approached it and a blonde head leaned out. Jeff bent forward and kissed the girl. His words were clearly audible to Kirk. "I'm sorry I kept you waiting, dear. Shall we go dancing?"

Simon didn't hear her reply. He didn't wait. Quickly entering the house, he shut the door behind him. For a man who was supposed to be a success, he was strangely unhappy. He tried to cheer himself up.

"I haven't any strings on her," he told himself. "Besides, if she'd been home, I'd have only made a complete fool of myself. I guess I should be grateful to Jeff instead of angry."

Simon went right to bed but his mental argument went on for hours. Finally, Morpheus gathered him into his arms and quieted the turmoil.

CHAPTER TEN

SIMON SAT outside the massive carved doors. His head was bowed and the cigarette in his hand went unheeded except for an occasional puff. His shoulders drooped and his red-rimmed eyes showed lack of sleep. He ran his fingers through his hair and glanced at his chronometer. It had been exactly five minutes since he had left the Council Room but it seemed like hours. His part was over; his plea had been made. Now it was all up to the Board. Behind those doors, they were considering it, deciding whether or not they would accept Simon's plans and, in so doing, decide whether or not Simon would become a member of the Board or a lone fighter.

In a short time he would know and then it would be all right. But the waiting was hard. Simon knew how futile it would be if he had to fight the corporations alone, yet, futile or not, that was what he would do. His thoughts strayed to Ellen. He had been a little shocked when he had seen her in the Council Room. She had smiled at him and had nodded encouragement but somehow it hadn't helped much. He had been more embarrassed than anything else. He wondered if she had seen him last night. "Oh well," he sighed. "Jeff's a good guy." But he'd said that a thousand times and it didn't do any good.

Kirk lifted his eyes at the sound of approaching footsteps. It was Jeffrey Davis. "Hello, Simon. Haven't they decided yet?"

Simon shook his head. Even though he didn't want to like Jeff, he did.

"Buck up, Simon," Jeff said, sliding into a seat beside him, "even if they don't like your ideas, I'm sure they'll give you the chair on the Board. After all, that's what they brought you here for."

"That's the trouble," Kirk replied. "The ideas go with me. If they don't like them, then I'm going back."

"But—why? Don't you like it here?" Jeff asked, amazed.

"That isn't the idea. If the Board doesn't see fit to abandon passivity, then I'm going to do what I can alone."

Jeff shook his head. "You'll have a tough fight on your hands. But maybe—." They lapsed into silence.

Kirk sighed. "I suppose, while you're here, I should congratulate you," he said.

"Ah—thank you very much," Jeff replied, "but what for?"

"I—was, ah—standing near your taxi—last night," Simon said, embarrassed, "when—you left my father's house."

"What are you driving at?" Jeff asked.

"I—you had a passenger," Simon stammered.

"Oh! You approve of my taste." Jeff smiled. "I must be sure and tell her about the compliment. She's the sweetest little woman in all the world and I don't see how I could get along without her."

"Ah—yes," Simon said, painfully.

"You'll have to come over sometime," Jeff continued. "We have a little Jeff now. Say, why don't you bring Ellen over some night for dinner?"

"Ellen?" Simon repeated, stunned, "ah—little Jeff?"

"Yes. Say...what's the matter?" Jeff asked. "You look a little strange."

KIRK JUST sat staring at Jeff. He tried to say something but all that came out was an inarticulate noise. Jeff looked at him with a frown of puzzlement.

"Listen," Jeff said, "there's a very odd expression on your face. What's going on?"

Simon moistened his lips. "Ellen, Ellen is—you—I mean—you—"

"What about Ellen?" Jeff asked quietly. "You know you don't have to worry about her. You've got her hooked."

"What...?" Simon asked with a slight gasp.

Jeff shook his head. "You're mixed up about something and how can I help you if you won't tell me what it is?" Jeff looked at Simon closely and then a grin spread over his face. He laughed outright. "I know what it is... You thought it was Ellen in that taxi last night...didn't you? No wonder you look awful."

"It wasn't Ellen?" Kirk asked slowly.

"Of course not."

"Ruth and Ellen look a good deal alike but you could never get the two confused. Whatever made you think it was Ellen?"

Simon shrugged his shoulders.

"Well, you don't have to worry about that girl. Do you know she's got a scrap book full of clippings and pictures of you? It's so heavy I can hardly lift it."

"Scrapbook?" Kirk asked, blankly.

"Sure," Jeff replied blandly. "You've had your picture in lots of newspapers and magazines. Our agents bring back bundles of literature whenever they return and Ellen's always one of the first to go through them. Don't tell her I told you, though. She'd never forgive me."

"Oh," was all that Simon could say.

Jeff smiled and laid a reassuring hand on Kirk's shoulder. Just then, the doors opened and the Board's secretary beckoned to Simon. "Dr. Kirk, we're ready," he said softly.

The palms of Simon's hands were wet as he stood before the long table. His father, a little to the right of the chairman, smiled encouragingly but the faces of the other Board members remained non-committal.

The chairman arose and read from a small slip of paper. "After due consideration of your proposals, Dr. Kirk, and after hearing the testimony of the witnesses, the Board has reached a decision.   First, we accept your proposals to actively promote and establish freedom and equality throughout the world. It is understood that the details for carrying out these proposals are subject to a majority action of the Board. Second, we accept your application for the position as twelfth member on the Board of Governors of Free City." The chairman laid aside the paper and stretched his hand across the table to Simon. "May I congratulate you and say I am glad that you are one of us."

Kirk shook the extended hand. He didn't trust himself to speak.   The chairman straightened and rapped the table sharply with his gavel. "Meeting is adjourned."

THE BOARD members milled around Kirk.   He kept looking over their heads or between them, frantically, to find Ellen. When he had the opportunity, Simon's father drew him aside. "Well, son, you made it. I'm very proud of you, and Ellen, too."

"Ellen?"

"She was one of the witnesses," the General explained, "and I wish you could have heard her. Before she ws done speaking she had the Board convinced right down to the last man that you were the person for the job. She was really on top of her game. If I were you, I wouldn't let a booster like that get away."

Kirk's smile slowly broadened. "Maybe you're right, dad. By the way, what do you have to do to get married around here?"

The General lowered his voice confidentially. "Well, if you're in a hurry, just see one of the Board members and he can fill out a certificate for you. Then, if you happen to be passing a church, just walk inside..."

Simon rubbed his chin thoughtfully.

"The *new* Board member," the General continued, "probably won't have any forms in his office yet but I understand there is an old ex-General on the twenty-third floor who has a desk just bulging with them."

Simon smiled at his father. "I haven't asked her yet."

"Well what are you waiting for?" the General asked. "Wait a minute. I've got an idea..."

Then General ushered his son out into the hall. "You wait here. Give me five minutes and then take the stairs up to the laboratory. I'll see that no one is there but Ellen. Then, you're on your own..." The General stepped into the elevator and the doors closed.

Simon paced up and down the hall. He rehearsed what he would say to Ellen. He looked at his chronometer and walked slowly up the stairs. He reached the upper hallway and walked toward the door marked:

BOARD OF GOVERNORS, SCIENTIFIC LABORATORY.

Simon was on the point of knocking when he remembered that no one would be there but Ellen. He decided not to knock and opened the door carefully and closed it with hardly a sound.

The office was deserted so he walked into the main laboratory. Ellen was studying something on a workbench. Simon had an impulse to leave. He couldn't do it. What he had planned on saying was all wrong. Besides, he couldn't remember a word of it. A feeling of latent panic seized him.

He turned to go and bumped into a table—a metal flask fell to the floor with a crash.

Ellen wheeled around. "Oh, Simon," she said. "I didn't hear you come in."

"Hello. Ellen," he said stupidly. "I—that is—you."

"I suppose your father told you about my speech," she smiled. "Well, it was only the truth, Simon, and you would have been approved by the Board anyway. I just said what anyone would have who knows you."

Kirk's knees felt a little unsteady as he walked over toward her. Nothing he could think of to say seemed rational.

ELLEN SLID away from the work, bench and stood up. "Well," she said brightly, "how does it feel to be a Governor?"

"Ellen..." Simon said softly.

She looked at him, startled. Her lip began to tremble and her eyes widened. "Yes...?"

Simon took a long breath. She was looking at him in that certain female way. "Ah nuts," he said to himself and took her in his arms. He held her close. "I love you, Ellen," he whispered in her ear. "Will you marry me?"

Her hair brushed his cheek, as she nodded. As he held her, little tears began to trickle down his neck. "Oh, Simon," she whispered. "I was afraid you might not ask me."

"I was afraid you'd refuse," he murmured.

Later, in the General's office, Simon and Ellen stood before the General's desk. The General had been busy and the place was filled with Simon's friends. Everyone was in high spirits except Wingate, who was strangely solemn and silent. As soon as the General affixed his signature to the certificate, Simon and Ellen were hustled out of the room. Everyone insisted on going with them to the church, everyone, that is, except Wingate. As the elevator carried them toward the ground level, the Captain blew his nose loudly. Ellen looked at him sharply. Tears were streaming down his ruddy cheeks.

"Why, Captain...what's the matter?" Ellen asked, sympathetically.

"I can't help it," Wingate blubbered. "Weddings always make me cry..."

"Ha!" MacNair grunted.

From the look on MacNair's face, Simon could see that Wingate would not be allowed to forget this for years to come. Then Simon looked back at Ellen and all at once there wasn't anyone within a thousand miles of them. They didn't even see the doors open at ground level.

CHAPTER ELEVEN

SIMON awakened to an insistent buzzing sound. It was the urgent signal on the 'visor beside his bed. His hand groped forward and snapped the set on.

A young man's face appeared on the plate. "This is the Monitoring Station, Dr. Kirk. We've just picked up a message that may be important. It's ultra-high frequency audiovisual but it's scrambled." The young man paused...

"Couldn't it have waited until morning?" Simon asked, wearily.

"I don't know," the young man answered. "Our coordinates show that it originated on a small island not more than a hundred miles from here. We think the message was beamed to Power City although, at that distance, we can't be sure. We've got both halves recorded and we're trying to unscramble them."

Kirk scratched his chin. "All right. Keep working on it. I'm leaving in a few minutes so forward any information to the Government Building."

"Right." The young man disappeared.

Simon dressed quietly, trying not to awaken Ellen. Just as he was ready to leave the room, however, she stirred. "What's the matter, darling?" she asked, half awake.

"Nothing dear. Just some business I have to attend to. I'll be back in a little while. Go back to sleep."

Ellen turned over and drew the blankets up under her chin. Simon stood over her for a moment, smiling and then bent over and kissed her forehead. Softly, he left the room.

Fifteen minutes later, Simon walked into the Government Building. As always, the interior was brightly lighted and it gave the impression that the building was teeming with life. Although this was highly improbable at that time of the morning, it was none the less comforting. Simon was now accustomed to the personalized atmosphere of the various buildings, so different from the lifeless monsters of Transinc, which became inert and tomblike when deserted.

Simon stepped into the elevator and turned to the metal grill set on the wall. "Forty-seven, please," he requested.

"Forty-seven," the metallic voice repeated. The voice, although originating from no human source, enhanced the feeling of companionship that the building engendered.

A moment later, Simon stepped out on the forty-seventh floor and walked briskly to his office. Inside, he settled himself at his desk and, touching a stud, activated his 'visor. "Relay all calls for Dr. Kirk to his office," he ordered.

"Understood," the 'visor answered tonelessly.

Snapping the 'visor off, Simon leaned back in his chair and stared at the ceiling, meditating. When he had first arrived in Free City, he had thought the vocal command relay systems in use were both wasteful and cumbersome. Now he had come to realize how much the little things enriched a man's life. He tried to count the different devices the city was using just to make life interesting and entertaining.

THE 'VISOR chimed melodiously and Kirk straightened in his chair. He snapped it on and a middle-aged man appeared on the screen. "Dr. Kirk, we have an urgent message."

Simon nodded.

"T-338 under Captain Wingate. Emergency landing in ten minutes. Captain requests immediate audience with Board of Governors."

Kirk frowned. "All right," he assented. "Have the crew come to the Government Building. I'll try to get everyone together."

Half an hour later, the Board of Governors was assembled in the Council Room. Wingate, MacNair, Bryant, Anderson, Barronoff and Markham sat in a row, ill at ease, while Kirk gave a rapid summary of the events that led to his calling the meeting. Then, turning to Wingate, he said, "I guess it's your turn to speak, Captain."

"Thank you," Wingate rumbled. "Well, it all began like this. I proposed to my friends yesterday morning that we do a little scouting around, purely for the purpose of improving our knowledge of this area, you understand. Well, we discussed this with Mr. Bryant at the airfield automat. 'Bryant, my boy,' I said, 'I feel it would be to the advantage of the city if we—' "

MacNair leaped to his feet. "I'd much preferrr ye dinna wearrr oot yourrr vocal cords.

The chairman of the Board rapped his gavel sharply and glared the two men into silence.

"Maybe I'd better tell what happened," Bryant said, quietly.

"Aye," MacNair replied.

Once again the chairman pounded the gavel. The room became still.

"THE SITUATION is roughly this," Bryant began. "We landed on the island, designated as C-14 on our maps and I guided our party along the beach, intending to show them the cave the city is planning to use for ship storage. Just as we reached the cave, we were assaulted by a group of armed men. They took us into the cave and held us captive for several hours. There was a ship in there but none of us had seen that particular design before. It was painted dull black and had no insignia or numbers on it. The men who captured us seemed to be waiting for someone and, after about three hours, a man who we think is their leader came in. He questioned Captain Wingate but the Captain refused to answer any questions. The man left us then and went into the ship. I saw the ship's beam antenna rotate a little so I supposed he was communicating with someone. He came out in a few minutes and ordered us released. We made our way back to the ship, made sure they weren't following us and returned as quickly as possible."

Simon came to his feet. "That must be the message the Monitoring Station recorded."

The other Board members stared at him curiously. In brief sentences, Kirk explained about the message and his reason for being at the building at such an hour.

A hurried conversation with the Monitoring Station disclosed that they were doing their best but it would take another half hour. The Board sat back in their chairs to wait, asking questions of the crew.

Finally, the large screen in the conference room lighted and a line appeared on its surface, dividing the screen into two halves. A dark, beetle-browed man with receding forehead came into view on the right half. "9 calling W. B.," the man said. He repeated this several times.

Then a portly gray-haired man appeared on the left side of the screen. "Go ahead, 9," he ordered.

"We picked up some men who were prowling around the beach," the man known as 9 began. "They came in a Transinc explorer, Number T-338. My men held them here for three hours until I arrived. One of them is named Wingate and I think he is the Captain. I believe I've seen him at Transinc. In fact, I'm certain."

W. B. LOOKED downward. "Just a minute," he said. He disappeared and returned almost immediately. "A report went out some time ago that he had crashed while commanding that ship. So it must be Wingate."

"What shall we do with them?" 9 asked.

"Under the circumstances, I think they must be spies but we can't take the chance. If they are spies, it means Transinc is getting wise to us or they might be looking for a place to set up a military base of their own. Ah—this is what you'd better do. Tell them you're sorry you detained them and let them go. Then, tomorrow night, and each night after that, cruise over the adjoining islands. Check them for infrared and all kinds of radiations but, most particularly, take a picture of each one. Flash the pictures to me and I'll check them against the surveys. If they've got a camouflaged base, it will show up. By the way, when they leave, try to get a general idea in what direction they go. It might help."

"What do we do if we find something suspicious?" 9 asked.

"Just drop a bomb," W. B. smiled. "One of the Mercury disintegration types will do."

"Okay, Chief," 9 said, "but what about your end? Won't there be some questions asked?"

"I doubt it," W. B. answered. "If Transinc has established a military outpost, they wouldn't dare do anything. If, on the other hand, Wingate is on his own and Transinc doesn't know about him, no one will ever miss him. Don't contact me again until you have something definite. It's too risky."

"Right."

Both screens went blank. The men in the room stirred uncomfortably. The 'visor lighted again and the face of the Monitoring Station Superintendent appeared. "Did you get it all, gentlemen?" he asked.

"Yes, we did, thanks," Simon answered. "If you pick up anything else give us a flash."

The Chief Monitor nodded and disappeared.

General Kirk arose and addressed the chair. "Gentlemen, this is *it*. This is what we've been expecting for years. We have some very grave decisions to make but I think we need a little time to collect our thoughts. I suggest we adjourn until 600. That will give us a chance to do some thinking and have breakfast."

The chairman glanced at the other Board members questioningly. With slight nods, they indicated their approval. The chairman rapped the gavel and adjourned the session. The members filed slowly out of the room. The usual conversation was absent.

The General and Simon walked together but they didn't speak until they reached the elevator.

"Have you got any ideas?" the General asked.

"Not a one," Kirk replied, "at least, nothing definite."

They rode down in the elevator, lost in their own thoughts.

"Would you like to have breakfast with us?" Simon asked his father when they reached ground level.

"Not this morning," the General answered. "I've got a number of things I must attend to."

"All right, dad," Simon sighed. "I'll meet you in the Council Room then."

SIMON walked rather rapidly and reached his home in a very few minutes. As he opened the door a savory mixture of breakfast smells greeted him. Ellen met him halfway to the kitchen. She kissed him and ran her hand across his furrowed brow. "Poor Simon," she murmured.

"Not poor Simon," he corrected. "Poor Free City."

"What's happened?"

Taking her arm, Kirk guided her to the table. Between mouthfuls of food, he explained the developments.

"So what are we going to do?" she asked.

"I don't know, but we've got to do something. It's just a question of time now before we're discovered. Why don't you come along with me to the meeting? We can use all the brains we've got."

"I don't want to interfere."

"Don't worry, darling," Kirk said, smiling. "There isn't anything you can do to make things worse."

"Maybe you're right."

"You'll come then?"

She smilingly nodded. "To give you moral support."

Throughout the rest of the meal and until they left the house, Ellen tried hard to dispel Simon's gloom. She had partly succeeded by the time they reached the Government Building. The General was waiting for them by the elevator. "How are you feeling?" he asked.

"Just the way you do," Simon answered. "Maybe a little more so."

"Coming up with us?" the General asked Ellen.

"Yes," Simon replied before she could answer. "I asked her to sit in."

"That's a good idea," the General sighed. "She usually has something worth hearing."

It was a trifle past 600 when the chairman rapped for silence. "Gentlemen, I realize there's no need to repeat to you what is facing us. I propose we turn our meeting into an open forum."

Everyone nodded agreement.

"It seems to me," Dr. Belcourt said, "that we might settle this problem point by point."

"What do you mean, Doctor?" the chairman asked.

"I mean," Dr. Belcourt explained, "we all know that although our screen over the city prevents our detection from the standpoint of radiations, that same screen changes the island's typography. It's a veritable certainty that if we do nothing, we will be found and destroyed. We have detection equipment whereby we are warned of the approach of any type of craft. We have devices that would enable us to destroy or capture any ship that might come here. The question is then, should we capture such a ship, destroy it and its crew, or allow it to return to its base?"

"I would say capture it," the General answered.

"That would only be prolonging the inevitable," Dr. Belcourt answered.

"True," the General agreed, "but after all that's what we need most of all...more time."

"How much time would it give us?" the chairman asked.

"About a week, conservatively, and maybe as long as a month," Dr. Belcourt answered.

The chairman turned to the other board members. "Are there any other comments on this?" He waited and then called for a vote. Unanimously, the Board agreed to the capture of the ship when it arrived. The details were given to General Kirk, who left the room shortly in company with Dr. Belcourt.

The discussion continued until 1000 revolving around the same points and extending itself not at all. The chairman finally summed it all up. "I'm afraid we're just going in circles, gentlemen. Shall we adjourn until this afternoon? We can all keep in touch with General Kirk's office so that a meeting can be called at any time."

"I think it's a good idea," one of the members sighed, stretching in his chair. "I'm going home and talk it over with my son. He's always thought he could handle my job better than I do. Maybe he's right."

A low chuckle ran around the room. Slowly, one by one, the members left, Simon and Ellen being the last. As they went out, she clutched his arm tightly. "Oh, Simon, it all seems so helpless." Ellen said, biting her lip. She buried her face in his lapel. A moment later she straightened. "I'm sorry, dear," she apologized. "I don't want to add to your worries."

Simon smiled encouragingly and guided her out of the building.

When they reached the street, Ellen asked, "What would you like to do, dear?"

Kirk hesitated. "I—think I'd like to take a trip. Let's go to the same places you took me to on my first day here."

This cheered Ellen. "All right, darling," she agreed.

They stopped and had lunch at the small automat near the airfield. From there they went from place to place, almost methodically. Simon stopped occasionally to contact the General's office. When they reached the Archives Building, Ellen stopped suddenly. She looked at Simon, tears welling in her eyes. "Simon," she sobbed. "What's the use of going on. It isn't the same. It's all going to be spoiled. This building doesn't mean anything anymore. Those things inside are just words. They don't mean anything, either. It's all just a dream, a dream that won't quite come true."

Simon held her and stroked her hair without answering.

Finally Ellen turned her face to his again. Simon kissed her, holding her tightly. Then he looked into her eyes. "It's our dream too," he whispered, "and it's got to come true. I'll make it come true." Kirk's face was grim and determined.

Ellen had never seen that look before. Then the look softened and he kissed her again.

"Come on," he smiled. "Let's go inside."

Ellen followed him, quite happy, quite content, confident that somehow some way Simon would find a way.

Simon was not inwardly confident. For the first time in his life, he was experiencing the torturing doubts that are the inevitable companion of responsibility. As he walked through the rooms of the Archives Building, he thought of the people who depended on him. "What am I going to do?" he asked himself. "I've got to think of something...*and fast!*"

CHAPTER TWELVE

SIMON AND Ellen reached the document room, the same room in which Simon had promised Ellen that he would not leave Free City. Neither of them spoke. They just browsed. Suddenly Kirk glanced at his chronometer. "It's getting about that time again," he mumbled.

"Why don't you stay here?" Ellen suggested. "I can call your father for you."

"All right," Simon answered.

After Ellen had gone, Simon just stood, seeing nothing. His mind wandered over the same old ground, around and around in the endless circle it had traversed so often before. Then Simon realized he was staring at a picture of a rather kindly faced man.

"I wonder what you would say if you were here now." The expression on Benjamin Franklin's face remained unchanged and impassive. For a moment, Simon had the illogical impression that the real Franklin was looking at him across the ages through that picture. He glanced downward to the quotations beneath the picture, reading half aloud.

" 'A penny saved is a penny earned.' 'A word to the wise is enough.' " Simon drew a deep breath then and said, "Well, Dr. Franklin, now that General Howe has taken Philadelphia, what do you have to say?"

Simon imagined what Franklin might have said. "I beg your pardon, sir—*Philadelphia has taken Howe.*"

Simon's eyes twinkled. "Unbeatable old codger," he muttered. "Philadelphia has taken—" Simon's mouth closed; his brow furrowed. For several minutes he stood staring blankly, his mind deep in thought. He didn't notice Ellen when she returned until she touched his arm lightly.

"What's the matter dear?"

He turned. "Ellen, I think I've got it…"

"Got what?" she asked.

"Philadelphia! I've got it…"

"You what?" Ellen exclaimed.

"Come on. We've got to get out of here."

Simon rushed her out of the building before Ellen could press him for details. He was grinning when they reached the street, grinning broadly.

"A child could have thought of it," Simon chuckled, as he started a taxi.

"Simon, what is it?"

"It's perfectly clear," he explained. "You see; Philadelphia has taken Howe… No—no! I mean—oh, quiet now and let me think."

Kirk's brow became corrugated with lines of concentration that remained until they reached the elevator in the Government Building. In the elevator Simon nodded and muttered, "Yes, it'll work. I know it'll work…"

ELLEN HAD given up trying to get anything out of him. It took twenty minutes to assemble the Board of Governors. It seemed like twenty years to Ellen. Simon wouldn't even look at her. He sat in his Board chair, scribbling some notes on a pad, chewing on the end of his pencil occasionally. Finally all of the members settled themselves and the chairman rapped his gavel for silence. "Dr. Kirk, the floor is yours," he said.

Simon stood up slowly, wiping his palms on his trousers. He stared at the notes he had made and then looked up. "I— I don't quite—know how to begin this. Maybe I should say that I think I've found a method to save Free City and accomplish our objective of re-establishing the precepts of individual liberty throughout the world."

The Board members shifted a little in their chairs.

"First," Simon continued, "I'm going to ask our production coordinator, Mr. Mooring, whether or not a workable monetary system could be set up in Free City?"

Mooring looked at Simon and shook his head.

"Why?" Simon asked.

"The oversupply of merchandise, food and all other things would render an arbitrary medium of exchange worthless. Under efficient production, such as we have, no unit of exchange could be maintained at a reasonable value. It would be so nearly without value that it could attain no psychological value. People would regard it as being worth practically nothing. Stabilizing the value at a high figure would cause production increases that would exceed the demand. Then you would have to devaluate the trade unit or reduce the people on the island to relative poverty. It's a known fact that the unit of exchange cannot be materially greater in value than the commodity it buys. It could only be made to work here by shackling our production or destroying our too-efficient machinery."

Simon nodded, smiling. "I would like you gentlemen to keep this fact in mind." He paused. "My second point is this...a long time ago, there was a country called Cathay, later named China. This, country was overrun by conquerors more times than I can remember. Yet each time the conquerors disappeared and China remained."

"Are you suggesting that we absorb the rest of the world?" one of the members asked incredulously.

"Not exactly," Simon replied. "I *am* suggesting that we allow the rest of the world the opportunity of being absorbed by our advanced knowledge. In the case of China, gentlemen, the system was simple and automatic. China had a language, an alphabet, and scientific knowledge—particularly in medicine, mathematics and the other foundations that make up a civilization. The conquerors, on the other hand, were not as far advanced, so they readily accepted the advantages of Chinese culture and knowledge and, in so doing, they became, to all intents and purposes, Chinese. Even racial differences break down before the leveling influences of a superior culture."

KIRK GLANCED again at his notes. "Many people," he continued, "have the mistaken idea that China absorbed other nations by her sheer size—but that is an error. The size is a result of the absorption, not the cause. Cathay was a very small country at her beginning. The Ancients used to say, 'as a man thinks, so is he,' and this was exactly the case with China. When people began to read, write and talk like Chinese, they became Chinese."

Kirk was staring straight at Ellen as he talked. It was if he didn't dare look into the faces of his fellow Board members for fear he would lose his courage.

"It came to me suddenly," he went on, "that we in Free City are in exactly the same position as was Cathay. Rather I should say we are in a better position since we know that the world's economic system must break down under the impact of our technology. Isn't that right, Mr. Mooring?"

"If you could get the world to *use* our technology," Mooring answered.

Simon smiled. "I think that angle is already taken care of. The five companies operate on the principle of profits and the more efficient they become, the greater the profit. I'm betting they couldn't resist our new methods. They would want them so greedily that we could use them to bargain for our own security."

"Just how do you mean?" the chairman interrupted.

"I mean, we could offer our complete new technology to the companies and, in return, we would ask to be re-instated or assigned to one of the companies with all rights and privileges of the other employees."

"I don't see that it's much of a victory," one of the Board members commented.

"That's the subtle part," Simon answered. "Let's consider the outside world. Every man and most of the women spend between five to seven hours, six days a week, working and obtaining little more than the necessities of life in return. At this time, I think we have not quite seven hundred fifty thousand people in Free City. From this, you can see that if we went back, every person in the world would have an opportunity to hear from one of us a first-hand description of what our life was like on this island. In effect, our people would be ambassadors from paradise. Dissatisfaction would spring up where now there is only complacency. At one end of the scale, we have the breakdown of the companies' economic system and, at the other end, we show the individuals what life *could* be like. It may be an unjustified assertion, but I think that within two or three years of the time we went back, the world would be completely changed."

Simon fell silent and for the first time looked at the other members of the Board, uncertain.

Dr. Gaines, the psychologist of the Board, spoke. "Mr. Mooring has already rendered the opinion that, economically, Dr. Kirk's plan is sound. From a psychological standpoint, it seems to be more than that. In fact it might prove to be infallible. I could almost guarantee that the companies would rush to get their hands on our technology. As Dr. Kirk put it, they just 'couldn't resist.' On the other end, the plan would work just as inevitably, yet there is one point that has not been touched upon. When the company system deteriorated, someone would have to reorganize the society, get things going again, or complete chaos would result. This, of course, would be our job. We'd have our hands full at first—immeasurably so. But if we work hard and let the people know exactly what has to be accomplished, and then instruct them on how to do it, it wouldn't be too terribly long, in theory at least, before things would be…well…running rather smoothly. Eventually the whole world would be just like Free City is today.

"Keep in mind though, while I feel fairly certain that Dr. Kirk's plan will work, I'm making it sound, quite obviously, far more simple than it actually is. It will take tremendous work and planning—and all in a very short amount of time. But I suspect with the full power of this Board behind it, as well as the efforts of our citizens, that there is a solid chance for success. I'd like to add that perhaps the greatest day of my life was the day on which I cast my vote for the inclusion of Dr. Simon Kirk to this Board."

THE SILENCE deepened. No one moved. It was as if no one was even breathing. A plan, a momentous plan was before them, which might be the city's only hope.

The chairman rose. "Dr. Kirk, as you know we haven't the authority to say yes or no to your plan. The only thing we can do is have you offer it to the citizens and let them decide. We can, however, offer you our support. First, I wish to offer you my post as chairman of the Board as a token of my faith in you. I shall support you all the way and I feel fairly certain…" The chairman glanced around at the other members, many of whom nodded in assent. "…that the other members will, too."

Simon moved dazedly to the chairman's rostrum and looked self consciously at the other members.

Simon's father stood up, smiling. "Mr. Chairman," he said slowly, "I move that the communication channels be cleared so that you may speak to the citizens of Free City and call for a popular vote."

Another member rose to his feet. "I second that motion."

"It's—been—moved—and—seconded—"

A chorus of ayes cut off the balance of Kirk's remarks. Whatever else Simon was going to say was lost as Ellen ran forward and threw her arms around him. "I'm so glad I married you," she exclaimed, just before she kissed him.

CHAPTER THIRTEEN

"GOLLY!" Billy breathed. "What a guy!"

"Yeah, he was," Gramps agreed.

"And he wasn't far wrong in that estimate of two years either. After some careful negotiations, the companies let them come back all right and, for about three months, everything went along just as before. Then, little by little, things began to change. The first thing was the working day. Those machines and ideas that the folks in Free City brought with them started piling up little surpluses of this, that, and the other thing in warehouses. Finally, a year and a half after the Free men came back, the work day was only two hours long. But upstairs, in the management sections, the work was getting worse and worse. One little thing after another would go haywire. The labor credit value was going up and down like a rubber ball. Production methods were changing. Commodities were changed and redesigned. Clothes for instance. At one time, Fabrinc made them so they would last quite a while. Toward the end, they started making them so they could be worn one day and thrown away."

"But why?" Billy asked. "Why make clothes that cheap?"

"To keep production up, Billy," Gramps answered. "They tried their darndest to keep things going. Course there wasn't much trouble in the average worker's life. The prices were fluctuating like mad but they caught on to that pretty quick. If a box of breakfast cereal cost ten labor credits one day and one credit the next, they'd buy them up when they cost one credit and wait until they got cheap again before buying any more."

"Must have been awful, Gramps," Billy said.

"Oh, it wasn't too bad," Gramps smiled. "Since people were only working a couple of hours a day, they had time on their hands. They kept hearing from the people from Free City how beautiful the island was, so one day a bunch of men got together and tried planting some flower seeds. They went way out to the edge of Cominc and marked off a little square at the desert land and each day they'd come out and tend it, water it and care for it. Pretty soon the flowers began to grow. The years had dissipated the deadly radiations in the soil and, after a while, planting flowers became a regular pastime. People began to rediscover the thrill of seeing something growing that they had planted themselves.

"By this time, though, the Directors and bosses were growing gray-headed trying to keep their companies in one piece, but the break had to come sometime. One day, the Director of Cominc came out of his office after having worked all night and he saw people walking around, going places and enjoying themselves and looking as though they didn't have a care in the world. It was then that this man realized that they actually didn't have a care in the world. You know what this fellow did, Billy? He turned around, went back upstairs and told the other members of the Board of Directors that he was through, that he had had enough to last him the rest of his life so he was retiring. The news traveled like wildfire. Pretty soon, there was a whole wave of resignations when the executives realized they were killing themselves trying to save their companies when in reality the companies were already dead.

"THERE WAS a little period in there when it looked like everything was going to pieces but you should have seen the people from Free City pitch in. They worked hard and they were working for something they had dreamed about. Now that the companies were gone, they had a free hand and boy did they use it. They talked to people on the 'visor, got in and ran the factories, stopped people on the streets and talked them into helping their efforts and finally, after they'd gotten the idea across with everybody in all the cities, they arranged for the first election. After the election, things really began to run smoothly. Things got more efficient. And as far as I know, nobody ever did outlaw the labor credit system. They just stopped using it, just like Kirk expected.

"Simon Kirk went back to Free City eventually. He and some friends installed machinery and got it in working order again. Then they offered it to the world as the new center of government. It took a little time but finally a workable setup for world coordination was made and it was a pretty big date when they took over Free City. Before you were born, Billy, they changed the name to Kirkland. Simon Kirk objected to it at first, but it didn't do him much good. I guess people are still people, Billy. When they make up their minds to something, they're going to have it and they won't take no for an answer."

Gramps heaved a sigh and stretched in his chair.

"How come, Gramps, you never told me about this before?" Billy asked.

"Well, I guess maybe I'm not too proud of what I've done. My contribution to the world was a pretty negative one." Gramps looked intently at one of his hands. "You see, Billy, when Simon Kirk came back from Free City, I was the Director General of Cominc. My only claim to fame is I was the first man in an executive position to stop beating my head against a stone wall."

"Gee, Gramps!" Billy exclaimed. "You mean *you* were one of the last tycoons?"

"Yup, I sure was." The old man lapsed into silence.

"There's something I don't understand, Gramps," Billy said, slowly.

"Oh?" Gramps looked up. "What's that?"

"Well," Billy said, thoughtfully, "how come nobody ever tried living this way before they set up Free City?"

Gramps chuckled. "That's the funny thing, Billy," he answered. "This is probably the oldest kind of government there is. Every time a man gets married he sets up a little government based on the same ideas. A long time ago, so far back in history that nobody knows much about it, little groups of people lived this way. Along about the time I was born, though, the idea of brotherhood and fraternity among people interfered with the plans of us tycoons so we thought up a way to get around it. We gave this kind of government a name and made everybody afraid of that name with propaganda. We didn't tell people why they should be afraid of it, we just told them that they should be afraid. We used that ugly word to batter down everyone and everything that stood for liberty, equality and fraternity. We used that word to such good advantage that we almost wrecked the world."

"What word, Gramps?" Billy asked. "You mean Fraternal Government?"

Gramps chuckled again. "Nope, that wasn't it, Billy. In those days, we called it Communism."

THE END

If you've enjoyed this book, you will not want to miss these terrific titles...

ARMCHAIR SCIENCE FICTION CLASSICS, $12.95 each